JAMESON: A WINGS OF DIABLO MC NOVEL - NEW ORLEANS CHAPTER

RAE B. LAKE

ACKNOWLEDGMENTS

To Mr. Possessive - Even in this new place in life I know that you will move heaven and earth to protect what's yours. I appreciate all that you are and can't thank you enough for standing by my side.

To my little fighters- You girls aren't little anymore. The personality, the sass, the wit, the fight in the both of you makes me so proud even on the days I want to scream in frustration. Keep on fighting girls!

To my Friends, Family and Readers- Don't you think it's about time we figure out exactly what Archer and his boys are up to! Thank you for sticking with me though this journey and I hope you enjoy the story!

DISCLAIMER

This book includes several graphic traumatic events that may be troubling / triggering for some readers. Discretion is advised.

CHAPTER

JAMESON

"You slimy piece of shit! When I get my fucking hands on you, I swear to God!" I bark as I push my bike faster. The wind and light rain painfully splashing on my face as I follow Christian. We just wanted to talk to him. No actually, I was going to break his fucking hands for trying to cheat our club. Only we really did want to talk to him first. He must know that if I catch him that I'm going to break his fucking face, because the moment he saw me walking up to him at the exchange counter he took off. Now he's in his broken down hooptie of a car trying to fucking outrace me. My bike could easily catch up to him with no problem, but it was fucking drizzling and the roads were slick. The last thing that I want is to wipe out while trying to catch him.

I rev up and get closer to him, but the driver's window opens. I instinctively swerve behind the car. He is going to try to shoot me. It wasn't that damn serious, but now instead of just beating him down I'm going to have to blow his fucking head off. I duck down, getting as close to the body of my bike as possible as something flies out of the window—small shiny and red.

"What the fuck?" I briefly look down at the ground and nearly laugh out loud when I see that he is throwing chips out the window. The very same poker chips that he had been counterfeiting and ripping us off with, he is using as weapon. "You dumb fuck." In the back of my mind, I wonder if he thinks that by getting rid of the evidence it means we won't come after him or if he is truly trying to hurt me with large hunks of plastic chips? Either way I don't have time for this shit,

Archer had expected me back in the clubhouse at least an hour ago. As the VP of the New Orleans Chapter of Wings of Diablo, it's my job to get shit done quickly and quietly. Christian here shouldn't be giving me so much fucking trouble.

He throws another large batch of the chips out the window, they land in a pool in front of me. I ride over them, but the second I do, I know it's the wrong fucking decision. The slick plastic accompanied with the rain already on the road causes my front tire to slip to the side.

"Fuck!" In a flash I see myself going down. I was going to fucking crash, because of some goddamn poker chips.

The bike swerves back and forth before I can get a grip on it. I screech to a stop and Christian speeds away from me. I take in a few deep breaths after my near-death experience. I think it's only fair that Christian has one too. "Fuck this." I grunt, as I burnout to chase after him and catch up to him in a flash. If he wants to be a fucking dumb ass, then I will treat him like a fucking dumbass. I look around making sure that there are no police in the area and pull my gun out. They may have it all tied up with the police over there in the mother chapter, but here in New Orleans the Wings of Diablo MC is on the police chief's shit list. I fire a shot into Christian's back tire and hear him scream as his speeding car begins to swerve back and forth, fishtailing all over the place. The dumb fuck is still trying to get away.

"You're not going to fucking lose me Christian. Just stop the fucking car before you kill yourself." I yell at the man from a safe distance away. His screaming and the screeching of the tires let me know that he is not handling the car well. If he keeps this shit up it's going to flip, then I would have to dig his body out of the wreckage and explain to Archer why I had to kill him. It was bad enough that we had to watch our every fucking step with the local fucking law enforcement and riding around with dead bodies was certainly not smiled upon.

"Just fucking stop! Motherfucker!" I scream again as I hear the second back tire pop and see sparks shooting out the back of the car. Instantly I brake and fall back so I'm not caught in the wake of the out-of-control car. It's riding on the fucking rims right now. The car swerves one more time and finally skids to a stop in the dirt on the side of the road. I roll up to his window and reach in. He cringes away thinking that I'm going to hurt him. He's right.

I hit him with all I've got on the back of his head, like an errant child, "You stupid fuck! Is a couple of goddamn poker chips worth your fucking life? What the hell is your problem?" I yell at him; he just sits there crying like a baby. Obviously, he isn't a hardened criminal. "Shut the fuck up with all that crying shit. Get this fucking car back on the road and follow me."

"No ... I can't ... please don't kill me. I had no choice."

I roll my eyes and look back in the car, "I'm not going to fucking kill you. But if you try to run again, I promise you that I will." I stare him in the eyes so that he knows I'm telling the truth. I'm not going to be out here chasing this motherfucker all damn day.

"Ok. Ok, I'm coming." He nods his head. I pull off into the street and wait for him to do the same. It's a slow drive since he has no back tires, but at least the sparks from his car light up the sky. I can't fucking wait to get back to the clubhouse and hear this shit.

Finally, after riding for what seems like fucking forever, we make it to the clubhouse. The large metal building has been my home for a few years now and I wouldn't have it any other way. This place and the people inside are my family—my unit. These people mean fucking everything to me.

I park my bike and walk over to the side of Christian's car. He is still in there blubbering like a little fucking girl. "For fuck's sake, shut up! Fuck, you know what the hell you did ... take your fucking licks like a man."

"Please, no, I can't. I promise I won't do it again. I'll find another way. I didn't have a choice. They are going to destroy my life if I don't come up with this money. Please you have to understand. Please." He begs me and part of me is incredibly fucking intrigued by what the fuck he is saying. Who the hell has such a fucking grip on him that he is willing to go up against us? Did someone put him up to this? I'll have to make sure that I'm in the room with Yang when he questions him. Yang is so much better at that shit than I am. See me, I just want to punch him in the face until he talks. If he doesn't, then at least I get the satisfaction of knowing that I punched his goddamn teeth down his throat. Yang uses much different methods.

"Let's go. I don't have all damn day." I reach in and grab him by the collar, working to pull him towards the front doors of my club.

He drags his feet every fucking step of the way. "Please." He begs again.

"It's not me you need to be begging kid, you going to want to save all the strength you have left for Bones. He's not a very forgiving man." I laugh even harder when Christian starts to whine and cry louder. He probably thinks Bones is going to torture him. He might. Oh well, that's his problem then.

I go to open the front door. Only Yang actually opens it from the inside first, meeting me in the doorway.

"I'll take it from here." He reaches up and grabs the man from my grip.

"What the fuck? Is there a reason that you won't let me in?" I ask him, ready to jump down his throat in a fucking instant. I'm the VP there is no one in this fucking place that can stop me from doing anything except for fucking Archer.

"Yeah, there is a reason. You got business to handle Jameson."

"Business? What fucking business do I have to handle? Cause last I checked, the man who's neck you are holding onto is my fucking business."

"Yeah, well you got more business." He shrugs and points behind me.

I turn, my eyes following the direction that he is pointing. I have to squint to see what he means, but when I see the blonde wavy hair, I know exactly who it is.

That bitch.

CHAPTER

2

JAMESON

"What the fuck are you doing here? I've told you a million fucking times to stop fucking showing up here!" I growl at Monica, my entire body surges with fucking rage. I hate her. Fuck, I hate her, but boy did I fucking love her. Monica is my ex-wife. She was the one that I'd sent all my fucked up emails to when I was deployed. She was the one I'd jerked my fucking meat off to when I was out in the field for months on fucking end. She was the one that I had thought I was going to have my kids with. She was everything to me, but it wasn't the same for her. I came home early after an eight-month tour to find her in bed with the fucking grocery store manager. She'd been fucking him when I was fighting for my life, trying to make sure that I got home to her in one damn piece.

"Jameson, don't talk to me that way. I just wanted to come see you, is that so wrong? Can you blame me? I miss you." She tries to push her hands around my neck, but I stop her immediately. I don't want her to fucking touch me.

"I don't give a fuck if you miss me. We are fucking over. Remember I signed all the fucking papers and gave you all the money that you'd wanted. Now get the fuck out of my life." I stare her down for a second and turn to leave. I hope she gets the fucking picture this time around.

"Jameson, please!" She screams out for me and I can hear the tears. I hear them before I even turn back around.

"Please what, Monica? What the fuck do you want from me?" I charge her and grab her hard by her arms. How the fuck can she be here crying in my face after she tore me to fucking shreds all because she couldn't keep her fucking legs closed.

"I just want you to talk to me ... Please Jameson. You're all I have. You know you are. I fucked up. I'm such a horrible person. I just want to make it up to you. I want you to forgive me."

I shake my head, the fucking audacity. "Fine, you're forgiven." I say bluntly. Maybe this fucking tactic will work.

"Bull, I know you. It's going to take a lot more than that to forgive me. Tell me what I have to do, Jam. I need you. I miss you so much. Please ..." She tries to wrap her arms around my neck again, but this time I don't stop her. "I ache for you. So bad." She whispers as she presses her glossy lips hard against mine. She kisses me, and moans like it's the best fucking kiss she has ever had in her life. I can't say the same. In fact, it feels like nothing more than two dead fishes moving around against my face. She pulls back after a few seconds, a small smile on her face.

"Are you about fucking done?" I ask, there is nothing that she has won here for her to have that disgusting smirk on her fucking face.

"Jameson, why are you being so cold to me? I'm your wife."

"Ex! You are my ex-wife, because you couldn't wait until I got home from hell before you found a dick to ride." I scream right in her face, not even bothered by the fact that she is cringing away from me. She should be fucking scared of me. If I were any other fucking man and walked in on that scene, I would have fucking killed her. Instead, I just beat the shit out of him and let him walk the fuck out of my house. Monica and I had tried to stay together after that. She tried to convince me that it was a mistake and that she truly loved me. She had given me her whole sob story. She was lonely, and just needed someone in bed— a warm body, nothing more. I could understand that since I was lonely too. I wanted our shit to work so even after I walked in on that shit, I stayed with her. Despite that, every time she picked up the phone and I didn't know who she was talking to or every time she would wave hi to some man on the street, I'd question it. All I could think about was how many times she had fucked him while I was pining away like a little bitch wanting to get back to her. After just a few months, I began to resent her. There was no way for me to trust her again. Once that trust was gone so was the fucking relationship. I filed for divorce and gave her half of everything I had so she would get the fuck out of my life. She did just that too. Until she found out that I was in the Wings of Diablo. Now she wants to try to fix us. Now that she knows we are making bank with the casino she wants to be my woman again. Fuck that and fuck her. I can't trust her.

"You trying to tell me you think there is ever going to be someone who knows you better than I do? Huh, Jam? You think this is all my fault, you left me alone for all that time. Taking on tour after fucking tour. Never wondering for even a second about what the fuck I was going through." She screams back at me and jabs her finger in my chest.

I want to rip my fucking hair out. Is she really trying to tell me that her letting another man pound her out in our bed was my fault? This bitch is crazier than I'd thought if that is the case. "Then you should have fucking left me. You could have called me, sent a fucking email, snail mail, fuck send up damn smoke signals. You should have broken it off before I got home and had to walk in on that shit. That is what you should have done. If you really cared for me like you keep fucking saying that you do then that is exactly what you would have done!"

"Jameson, just listen-" She reaches out for me again, but I back away.

"Monica! I'm going to tell you this shit one more fucking time. Get the hell away from me. Stay the hell away from my club and get the fuck out of my life. I don't love you, and we are never getting back together. I don't fucking care what you have to say. So fuck off!" I stare at her, and even through the rivers of tears that are rolling down her face I don't let up. There is nothing that she can say to me or do that is going to change my mind. She had her shot and she fucked it up. Once you lose my fucking trust that's it.

"Jameson, please." She begs again, but I turn and walk over to the clubhouse leaving her and her fucking whining ass out on the front lawn. I didn't have time for her shit. I had more important business to tend to with my brothers.

CHAPTER

JAMESON

"I swear ... I can't tell you. I don't want any trouble with you guys. I never did, but this was the only thing that I could think of doing." Christian is sitting in the back room, tears and snot streaming down his face. Yang and Rags stand over him, but from the look of things they haven't even hit him yet.

"Everything good outside?" Yang turns to me, he knows how I get after Monica decides to pay me a visit. The woman always fucking puts me on edge. If there is one thing, I can say about her it's that she's persistent as fuck. No matter how many times I tell her to fuck off, I know that she is going to come back. It might be in a week or it might be in a fucking month, but I know for sure that this is not going to be the last time that I hear from her. She'll be back.

"Yeah. It's all good. What about this piece of shit? What is he telling you?"

Yang chuckles and turns back to him, "Nothing much, just been listening to him blubber like a fucking girl."

"Please, don't hurt me." Christian cries again.

"Hey, shut the hell up!" A hard voice rolls through the room. My head pops up and I look to Archer. I didn't even know he was fucking here. It's not unlike him to pop in on interrogations, but I didn't expect him to show up to this one. Usually anything that goes on with the casino he pretty much leaves to us. Archer isn't the biggest man, but he commands attention. He doesn't have to yell either. Just the tone of his fucking voice is usually enough to get bastards to do what the fuck he wanted them to do.

Christian tries to turn around and see who is talking, but he can't place Archer. He did stop the crying though which is a fucking blessing.

Archer walks up on the opposite side of him. Christian is so damn skittish that he nearly jumps clear out of his fucking seat when he turns to see him so close.

"Give me one reason why I shouldn't just kill you right now. Tell me why I should let you walk out of here."

The man's face instantly crumbles like he is going to start to cry again.

"And if you start that shit again, I swear to you I will put a fucking bullet in your mouth just to shut you up. Stop the fucking crying and talk." Archer stands back and crosses his arms over his chest.

"Ok, ok, I'm sorry. I'm not used to this. I'm sorry." Christian tries to get himself together.

"Who the fuck is making you counterfeit our shit?" Rags asks him.

"I can't tell you." Christian says.

Archer pulls out his gun and shows it to Christian, "I think you might have shit a little confused, you think that you have a choice here? Either you tell us what we want to know or we kill you. There is no in between. You sit here scared of someone else that might kill you when we are the ones with the gun to your head. Now let's try this again."

"Who is it?" Yang says.

"Can you promise you won't let him get me?" Christian asks. I can see that he means it. Whoever he is afraid of, he really is fucking afraid.

"I can't promise you shit, but I promise that I won't kill you." Archer says.

"Fine, fine. It's René." Christian says and his whole body drops, like all the tension has drained out of his body.

"René, ugh ... why does that man keep fucking coming up?" I look over to Archer who is standing back just staring up at the ceiling. René is someone who has been on our radar for quite some time now. He runs some kind of underground boxing club. He seems to be doing well for himself. Except more and more people are coming up either missing or in binds, because they are in debt to René.

"What exactly does he want with you?" Yang asks.

"I need to give him fifty thousand dollars. I have to get it to him by Saturday or he is going to force me to syphon off the medications that are meant for the community. He wants to sell them on the black market, cancer medications and shit like that. If I do that, I will lose my license and my job."

"What the fuck? What the hell is he going to do with that shit? I mean really how much does the medication actually cost that he thinks selling it on the black market is really going to do anything for him?" I ask not really understanding the need for cancer medications.

"Are you kidding me, there are certain medication that can go for ten thousand dollars a pop. Most of the time insurance will take care of it, but there are other times where people have to pay out of pocket for their drugs. If they can get it through backdoor sources, they will definitely do that. Listen I have family, kids. I can't go to jail and if I gave him the medication there is no way that I won't get caught. The system is fail proof and my signature would be all over it."

"So, you thought that you would come and rip us off instead?" Yang asks.

"It was the only other option, your chips are so plain. It didn't take long for me to make the replicas. I won't ever do it again. I'll find another way." Christian nods his head and when he sees that no one is reaching for their guns he continues, "I can help you guys out around here, I can do other things. I used to be heavy into forgery, but I haven't done that for a long time. I could do some stuff like that if you needed it."

"Hmm, I don't know. Seems like René has it out for you. We don't know if you are going to live long enough to actually be of any use to us." Yang shrugs and turns away.

"Rags, stay with him, make sure he doesn't get any ideas." I order and the rest of us walk out of the small back room. There was nothing more that Christian was going to give us. He was a low-level player, just doing what he knew how to do to make sure that his family still had him around. Of course, he had picked the wrong fucking mark. Though I can't really blame him for doing whatever he had to do to make sure that his family was taken care of. I'd do the same for my brothers.

"What do you think?" Archer asks me as Yang and I step out of the room.

"I think the bastard is telling the truth. There is no way with all that crying and shit that I think he is trying to pull one over on us. He is scared and this was his way out."

"So are you saying we should just let him go after he stole from us. What does that say about us? That we are so easily bested?" Yang asks, his eyes darting over to Archer.

Our president was calm and collected, but he was also probably one of the most dangerous individuals I had ever met in my life. He was also one of my closest friends and a brother in arms.

Archer was a sniper for the military, and I was his spotter. We went everywhere together and got in all the shit together too. He knew all about Monica and how I'd wanted to have kids one day when all my tours were finished. Yeah, I never cheated, but Monica was right when she said that I left her alone to go on tour after tour. Something about the freedom, when we weren't being shot at, had me mesmerized. I didn't realize that it had so much of an effect on her. I guess I didn't know her as well as I thought that I did.

Archer on the other hand I knew well. I knew how many times he bounced his leg when he had to use the bathroom, what every fucking long exhale meant, what he saw before he knew what it was, and I also knew that him shooting that little girl had broke a piece of him that he will never get back. When he'd left the unit, I didn't hold it over him. I knew that he was already dying inside and there was no way that he was going to be able to do his job.

"I'm saying that we can show a bit of mercy." Archer replies.

"Mercy? He stole from us?" Yang repeats.

"I know it. But we have more than we need and now we have more information. We know that our chips need to be changed since we know that they are easily forged. We have a new connection with someone who is a master at forgery. Honestly, if it weren't for the fact that the man was so fucking skittish, we would have never fucking noticed that he was playing us. Those chips are spot on." Archer speaks his mind and even if Yang wants to go in a different direction it's not going to happen. Archer may have asked for our input, but in this situation, he wasn't going to use it.

"What do you want to do with him in the meantime? I don't know if I feel right about sending him on his way knowing that he's got a big fish like René on his tail. You want to put him up?"

"Yeah, not here though. The last fucking thing I need is for him to try and forge something in here. Find out if he does keys and shit." Archer shakes his head, smirking slightly, "Jameson, I'll leave you to get shit set up. Make sure you get both him and his family somewhere safe until we get this shit with René straightened out."

I watch him walk away, but there is still one thing that is unclear. How the fuck are we going to find René? He is so deeply embedded in the underground that even I don't know what the man looks like. All I know is that folks are scared of him and are doing stupid shit to make sure that they don't owe him any debts.

"Archer, how the hell are we going to find him? No one even knows what the man looks like."

"I guess it's time we go hunting." Archer smiles and continues to walk away.

CHAPTER

CELINE

"Dad! Come on! Get your hands up!" I yell at the top of my lungs. The crowd full of people is roaring, but I know that he hears me. What I don't know is what the fuck he is doing? My father is one of the best fighters in the world, hands fucking down, and here he is letting this second-rate man pepper his face with jabs.

I see him look at me and a deep look of despair crosses his face. Usually when he is fighting my father is in the zone, all smiles all the way through. Right now, it looks like he hates what he does. I've never seen him look like this.

"Dad, what are you doing? Fight back!" I yell at him. When his opponent hits him with a hard right hook, I watch my father stumble backwards. I know something is wrong. I try to rush from my seat so that I can get over to where he is, but security stops me from crossing the line.

"Let me go, I have to get over there. Something is wrong. Can't you see something is wrong?" I yell at the man, but keep my eyes on my father. At thirty-seven years old my dad had pretty much aged out of the traditional boxing circuits, but he found a new crowd in underground boxing. They paid pretty well too, but nothing like the purse he would get if he were still with the professional circuit. The great part of it was, he has yet to lose a fight. He was the undisputed champion. He was fighting now like it was his first time ever in the ring.

The bell rings indicating that it was the end of the third round, and

I watch as my father slowly walks back over to his corner. He doesn't look like he is hurt or confused, he just looks sad.

"Dad!" I scream for him again and when he catches my eyes, I can see that his are watery. He looks like he is going to cry. What the fuck is going on?

"Sorry." He mouths to me before the bell rings again and he has to get up for the next round.

Sorry? Sorry for what?

His stance is completely off, and he doesn't even have his guard up. Why is he leaving his chin wide open? I get a good look at how he isn't even putting in minimal effort like he should be and I know why he is sorry. My father is going to throw this fight. He's losing on purpose.

"No! Dad, don't do it!" I scream at him and try again to push my way through security. Another guard has to come over and try to subdue me since I'm fighting so hard. I watch my father throw a ridiculously telegraphed haymaker, but before it could even make contact with his opponent the man crumbles to the ground dramatically.

"What the fuck?" The entire crowd goes quiet.

They all want to know the same fucking thing. How in the fuck did the man that was beating my father down the entire fucking match end up on the mat flat on his back?

"Booooo!" Everyone begins to scream and rant as they all feel like they'd just got swindled. My father is still the champ, but it's blaringly obvious that the man he just supposedly knocked out threw the fight.

I glance back up to my father and now the look of sadness is completely replaced with a look of shock, followed by fear and panic.

"Celine! Don't fucking move!" He screams and jumps over the ropes not even stopping to take off his gloves or wipe down the blood on his face. He barrels through the security guards holding me back and grabs my hands, together we start to run.

"Dad, what is going on?" I try to yank my hand out of his gloved hand, but he gets a better grip and keeps pulling me along.

"Keep up Celine! Fuck just keep up. I messed up bad. Shit! They played me!" We are still running, and he is out of breath. He isn't making any sense though.

"Who played you? What is going on?" I ask, but it's like my words go in one ear and right out the other. He isn't bothered with trying to explain anything to me right now.

When we make it outside, my father runs out into the middle of the street in front of a moving cab. Before it could even stop all the way he is pushing me in the back seat. He rattles off an address and the cab driver takes off all before I can get in a good breath.

"Dad for fuck's sake, what is going on?" I turn to look at the man that I have spent my entire life with. He'd raised me after my mom passed away. He was a teenage father who had nothing to offer me, except what he could work for with his hands. Fighting had put food in my belly. I'd never seen him scared. Now he is looking over his shoulders like he is waiting for someone to pop out of the shadows.

"Celine, I fucked up." He said again.

"What the hell does that even mean? How did you fuck up Dad? Just talk to me." I urge him.

"I've been gambling again. I know I told you that I would stop, and I was doing so fucking good for a while, but I got in deep. I thought that I would be able to dig my way out without you knowing, but it got bad."

I take in a few deep breaths and try to keep to my voice even. "How much do you owe Dad?"

"Two hundred thousand dollars."

My eyes nearly bug out of my head, "Two hundred! What the fuck! How the hell? Why?" I couldn't understand how the hell he would have gotten this deep into debt.

"I don't know baby, I'm so fucking sorry."

"It's ok. It's ok we can get it paid down. It'll take some time, but we can get it paid down."

"That is the problem. I was supposed to throw the fight. René said that if I didn't throw the fight that he would come for a different form of payment."

René? He is in debt with René even I knew that was the worst fucking possibility. René's son, Thomas had been trying to get with me for ages, but I never once allowed him to pursue anything with me. Thomas was what I like to call a weakling. Not that he didn't have any body mass or was sickly small. I was sure that if shit hit the fan, he would be the first one to cry and run to daddy. If I'm going to be with someone, it's going to be someone who I know is going to take charge and not shy away from a fight even if they know there isn't going to be anyone there to save their ass.

"What is the other payment?"

"Don't worry about it, don't worry. I'll make sure I get the money. We just have to get out of dodge for a little bit."

"Daddy! What is the other payment?" I ask again, the fact that he won't tell me is making me edgy. Does it have to do with me? Is that why he was so desperate to get to me after the fight was over? The man only now takes off his gloves. What the fuck is this about?

"René wants you for Thomas. He said that if I didn't throw the fight that he would take you as the form of payment."

The tears well up in my eyes, how could he do that? Why would he ever agree to have me as a stipulation as part of his debt repayment? "Daddy ... why?" My voice cracks with all the emotion. I knew my father loved me, but maybe it wasn't as absolute as I'd thought. The cab pulls up to a stop in front of our small house and we get out. Dad is still in his boxing shorts and no top. The gloves now tied together and hanging over his neck.

"Celine, I fought with him. Fought for them to pick something else. But it didn't matter there was no way that I wasn't going to throw the fight. I would give up my belt for you a million times over. They knew that and I think that is why the other fucker fell before he could swing the final blow. They set me up." His eyes stay on mine as he rubs his hand down my hair and over my cheeks. He is touching every part of me like he thinks I'm going to disappear. No, there is no one that could tell me that my father didn't love me. I knew that he did.

"They set you up, because they want me. This was always about fucking Thomas. That limp dick bastard."

"Please stop talking about men's dicks." My father says as he cringes and grabs my hand pulling me towards the house. I may be twenty-one years old, but he still gets uncomfortable talking to me about boys and shit like that. Typical father who doesn't think anyone is good enough for his little girl.

16

"What are we going to do?" I ask as he opens the door to the house, and we shuffle in quickly.

"We just need to get out of town for-"

The light on the far side of the room turns on and, in the chair, I see René. "Oh, no, please don't tell me the two of you are going to leave already? I mean that would be in such poor taste, especially since we had a gentleman's agreement. You are not trying to go back on your word are you, Lex?"

My father roughly shoves me behind his back. I'm sure he wants me to run, but I know that if I do they will shoot him. René has no qualms about killing anyone when it came to his business. There is no way that he would just let me leave and my father not pay the price for it.

"Fuck that, you played me. There is no agreement. You told me to stay on my feet until the fourth round, to throw a haymaker and let him counter to knock me out. That is exactly what I did, but your man went down."

"I guess you just don't know your own strength." René shrugs his shoulders and gets up from the side chair we kept by the couch.

"Are you out of your mind? I didn't fucking touch him. He went down on his own accord."

"Ah, well I don't know what to tell you about that. But the good news is your still the champ and I'm sure that there are going to be so many people coming for you to get a shot at the belt."

"I don't give a hot shit about that belt. You know that I was going to throw that fucking fight. I didn't agree to this." My father growls out and takes a menacing step towards René.

"I don't give a fuck what you were going to do. All I care about is my fucking money. The fucking debt that you owe me and that you will fucking pay in the way that we agreed on. I told you to throw the fucking fight or I would have your daughter for my son. Thomas' birthday is coming up and he is just dying to have the company of your daughter. It really won't be that bad. I promise you."

"Fuck you, you'll have to kill me first!" My father lunges at the man, but two guards immediately grab hold of him. Or at least they tried to. My father threw up his hands in perfect stance.

17

A quick three punch combo to the face of one of the guards is enough to knock him out. My father turns his head to the next guard and proceeds to knock him out too. It's not until I feel the cool steel pressing against my head that I realize my father won't win this fight.

"Lex, maybe you need to re-evaluate what the fuck you are doing?" René says from behind me.

René is a tall man, at least three inches over six feet. He has broad shoulders, deep wavy hair and a perfectly groomed beard. If it weren't for the streaks of grey at his sideburns, I would have never known he was an older man. I also didn't feel even one tremor in his hand. He was sure about his decision. If my father charged him, he would pull the trigger. I kept completely still as I watch the anger and determination drain from my father's eyes. He knew that he had to stop. He knew that he had to let me go in order for both of us to get out of this room alive.

"Celine ..." My name barely a whisper out of my father's mouth.

"It's ok Daddy, I'm going to be fine I promise you. I'll figure a way out of this." I say and give him a small smile. I need him to keep himself going. If I was going to find a way to survive whatever Thomas had planned for me, I need to know that dad will be okay.

He looks like he is resolved to let this happen, but then he shakes his head and tries again to get to René. "Please, just give me another way. Let her go, she has nothing to do with any of this. I promise you I will work double time. Do whatever you need me to do ... if you just let her go."

"Sorry, my Thomas has been patient long enough. She will make a fine birthday present for him. Besides you know how young people are, he's bound to get tired of her soon. She'll be back with you in no time. Just let him have his fun first."

I can't stop the whimper that comes out of my mouth. Fun? I can only imagine what his kind of fun is. I'm sure it is only Thomas trying to prove to everyone just how much of a man he really is.

"Fuck, no please." My father cries for the first time ever in my life. This is tearing him apart.

"Dad, be strong." I try to get him to focus. I need him to not do anything rash or anything crazy to force them to hurt him. If they hurt him there is no way that I would be able to survive.

"I think that's enough family bonding for now. Tell your papa you'll see him later." René moves the gun away from my head and makes sure to put it in a place that I won't be able to get to it.

"Dad, look at me." I try to put as much strength in my voice as I could. Sure, this was his fault and it was scary, but that didn't mean I couldn't get out of it. I was a strong woman. He'd taught me how to stand on my own two feet. I was a fighter. When his tear drenched eyes finally raise up to see me, I say, "I will see you later. Make sure you're still around you hear me?"

I want him to promise me that he's going to be ok. I don't want what is happening here to break him. I don't want him to lose himself just because he is without me for a while. He must stay strong so when I can make it out, I'll have him to lean on.

He wipes his eyes and stands up tall. "Ok, we can work this. I'm so sorry Celine ... I'm so sorry." He apologizes over and over as René turns me around and we walk out the door. I have no idea where he is taking me, but I know for sure it's not going to be a walk in the park.

CHAPTER 5

CELINE

The second I make my way into the fancy car that is waiting for René I know that my life is about to change for the very worst.

"Hurry the fuck up bitch!" One of the guards says as I slowly try to make my way to the opposite side of the seat. He shoves me across the seat with his foot.

"What the fuck do you expect me to do, fly?" I snap at him. René grabs me by the hair and yanks me halfway back out the side of the car.

"Oh sweetheart, I think you need to get a few things straight. You better watch who you are talking to. This isn't your home. You aren't talking to one of your friends. I promise if you keep the attitude that you have now, I will make sure that you don't get delivered to my son in prime condition. Know your fucking role, you're a pet, nothing more." He lets go of my hair and I fall down onto the floor of the back seat of the car. I wasn't used to having someone put their hands on me and not retaliating.

I have to bide my time though. I have to get through whatever the fuck this is if I want to survive long enough to get home.

We drive for a long while until we stop at a simple two floor house. It is a nice little house except inside instead of their being the normal furniture and knick-knacks, there are rows and rows of medical supplies. It's like a back house for doctors. I'm assuming that every-thing that takes place in this house is under the table. René walks in front of me and shoves me to a door, but he doesn't say a word.

"What do you want?"

He smacks me hard upside the back of my head like a parent would an unruly child. It makes me seethe, but I can't react. I have to just fucking take it. "Don't act stupid now. Go in the room." He answers me.

I open the door and in the room is a tall blond man with a white lab coat. I guess he is a doctor. He looks at me once, but there are no further pleasantries.

"Take your clothes off and get on the table." He motions to the plastic looking table that is in the center of the room.

"Why the hell am I taking my clothes off? Who the hell are you?" I recoil when I realize that he isn't going to give me any privacy at all.

"You are here for an exam, they are standard. Strip." The so called doctor says again.

"No. I don't need a physical." I reply before a thick strap connects with my backside.

I fall down to the ground, screaming out in surprise and pain as I watch a calm René standing over me with a belt wrapped around his hand.

"I can't believe I have to tell you this again so soon. You are nothing but a fucking pet. If. He. Says. Get. Naked. Then. Get. Fucking. Naked." He swings the belt down on my flesh as an exclamation with each word. I cry and try to get away from him, but he pulls me back and continues to beat me. After what feels like forever and I'm sure my skin is split open from the constant beating he stops. "Now, get the fuck up and take your fucking clothes off. You are already wasting my damn time." René snarls at me.

I do the best I can. Only my legs hurt so bad from the pain of him hitting me that I fall down a few times before I can get up and start taking my clothes off. When I turn my back, I can see that René is still in the room.

I hesitate for a second thinking that maybe he will leave. I would rather be alone to do this humiliating act that he is demanding, but he stays.

"Do you think I'm not going to examine the goods after I spent all that money on you. I want to see exactly what my son is going to get for that favor I blew." He crosses his arms and just relaxes against the door frame.

My body trembles slightly as I turn back to the doctor and take my clothes off. When I had nothing but my bra and underwear on, I hear René let out a huff. "I understand the draw. Not my particular taste though " I turn in his direction and he shrugs his head as he turns and walks out of the room. Apparently, his part of the examination was over.

"The under clothes as well." The doctor says tearing my eyes away from the door that René had just left out of.

"For what?" I say through my clenched jaw.

"Girl, please don't make me call him back in here. If you think the belt was bad, it'll only get worse from there. Just do what I'm asking of you. Take everything off. This is a full checkup."

I nod and at that moment I can see the exhaustion in the man's face. The deep dark circles that are under his eyes and the way he appears to not have any energy to fight with me. I would bet good money that the doctor is here against his will too. That this is some fucked up debt payment that he has to do.

"Ok, I'll cooperate, but can you just tell me why this is happening. What does he want me to be checked up for?"

"There was a slut brought into the inner circle that had HIV. She fucked her way through a lot of his men, some of them contracted the deadly virus while others did not. From then on, he likes to make sure that everyone on his team is in ideal health. It's mandatory that everyone be tested. At least once every three months." The doctor replies and completely nude I get up on the table, he grabs my bra and underwear and places them in a trash bag. I guess I won't be getting those back.

"I am also supposed to note any identifying marks or deformities that you may have. Anything where someone might have to do any upkeep with you." He continues to explain as he starts the portion of the physical exam that tests my neurological capabilities.

"Upkeep? I don't think I'll be around for upkeep. Once Thomas gets tired of me, he'll let me go." I say and even as I hear the words coming out of my mouth, I know how fucking naive that it sounds.

"Sorry kid ... once you're in, you're in to stay." The doctor finishes that part of the exam and pulls out an EKG machine, lays me down and attaches the electrodes to my body. I knew that everything was going to come back in tip top shape. My father always made sure that I had the best care. I don't think I have ever gone a year that I missed a checkup.

"Ok all that looks good, now come on and put your legs in the stirrups." The doctor says as I see him lubing up a metal speculum.

"Wait, I don't have any STDs or anything. I'm clean. I swear it." I'm fearful, because there is no telling how rough he is going to be. The last thing I want is my cherry to be popped by a fucking speculum.

"I have to do a pap smear." The doctor huffs, clearly pissed off that I was once again giving him a hard time.

"Look, I know you don't owe me anything, but can you just be gentle. I've never ..." I let the words die off and I see his face light up after a second with him catching the drift.

He places the speculum down and then picks up a smaller one, lubes that up and then sits on the small rolling stool between my legs.

"Ok, let me take a quick look. This will be fast." It's all very uncomfortable, but he is honest when he says it will be over fast. A few cell samples taken and a quick look around, then he is done.

"Thank you for that." I say knowing that this could have gone a whole lot worse.

"Don't thank me. I have done nothing but what I must. You can put your clothes back on." He turns and walks over to a small desk. He bags up the small test tubes with the samples and makes his notes in a small folder.

I make quick work of putting my clothes back on, without my panties or bra, and sit back on the table. I hope they wipe this down before each patient. The doctor gets back up with a few more tubes and another kit. He places them next to me on the exam table and I find myself cringing away from him. I hate fucking needles.

"I have to draw some blood and then you'll be all done. This is just the rapid test, but the blood test will be more conclusive."

I nod my head and wait for him to do what needs to be done. He swipes the q-tip around my mouth a few times before he places it in a small tube, closes it securely, and shakes the solution back and forth. There are about four blood tubes that he takes and just like before he is as gentle as he can be.

"What is your name?" I ask as he draws up the last tube of blood.

"Guppie."

"Guppie? Like the fish?" I say a hesitant smile on my face.

"Yeah, I guess my momma didn't like me." He shrugs as the same hesitant smile tries to bloom on his face.

"Are you fucking here to flirt with the dogs or are you here to work? Because I'm sure that we can find you so more fucking work to do if you need it." René stands at the door watching. Guppie turns and walks away from me, not even addressing what was just said. He wasn't flirting with me. He was just being nice, but I guess in René's mind that is one in the same thing.

"Where the fuck are her results?" René puts his hand out and Guppie places the same manilla folder that he was just writing in on his palm.

René opens it up and flips the page up. "Hmm, would you look at that. My boy got himself a fucking virgin. How fitting!" René drops the folder onto one of the side tables and saunters over towards me like a cat sizing up his prey. "It's a shame, your father could have gotten way more for you." He grabs my face by the chin, but I rip it away. I know I shouldn't be fighting right now, but I just can't help myself.

"But every gem has it's flaws, right? We are going to have to beat that rebellious streak right out of you. No worries, we have a couple of days before Thomas' big day. I'll make sure you are right as rain before that." René promises and smacks me hard against the side of my face.

I try not to glare at him. Although for the life of me, I know that whatever he has planned is going to leave me anything but right as rain. In fact, I'm almost positive that it's going to leave me more broken than I have ever been in my life.

CHAPTER

6

CELINE

It's been three days since I last saw my father. Every day I wake up expecting him to burst through the door and save me. I wait for him to jump through the window like fucking Spiderman and steal me away. It never happens and the longer I stay here the more I realize that he's never going to be able to do that. There is way too much security around for him to be able to do something like that. I would have to get out on my own or I would really be stuck here until Thomas was finished with me. That would never happen since Thomas is completely obsessed with me.

"Bitch!"

I have already become so accustomed to the word that it didn't even bother me anymore or the fact that I knew they were referring to me. I walk out into a small room where René and a few other men are sitting around, all drinking and smoking. There is a woman in the middle of the floor unconscious and bleeding. I don't know if she is dead or not, but she is clearly close to it.

I dart down to where she is and touch her, trying to help her.

"I'm glad you seem so interested in helping her, she left a fucking mess. Clean it up."

When I look down, I realize that mixed in with the puddle of blood is also vomit and shit. She must be dead. I was kneeling in all her filth.

"What in the shit?" I try to back out of the small area, but René snaps his fingers so that I will pay attention to him. I'm starting to pick up on the small cues and know what angers him. It's amazing how quickly someone can learn when it comes to survival.

"Clean it up." He orders me.

My head falls down and I roll my eyes in a matter that he can't see. I don't want him to notice anything that he can say is disrespectful.

I try to stand.

"Didn't you fucking hear what I said, bitch?" René growls at me.

"Yes, I heard you. I just need to get something to clean it up."

"Use your fucking hands." a slight smirk crosses his face and I see the dare in his eyes as he waits for me to fight back. I won't though. I know that they are just searching for an excuse to beat on me. So far, I have been more than lucky that none of them have tried to punish me sexually. I was going to try to keep it that way.

I look back down to the floor and the nastiness. I look at my hands and can't believe that I'm about to do this. I begin to use the edges of my hand and scrape the mess into a pile in the middle of the floor. There is a can in the room that I use to push the mess into. There is no way that I'm able to get the liquid mess completely off the floor. When I get the bulk of it in the can, I look at him to see what other humiliating tasks he has for me to do.

"I told you to clean it up." he demands, leaning up on the edge of his chair.

"I did. I can't pick up any more with my hands."

"Use your shirt then." One of his guests suggests as he sips on his drink and laughs. I look at him with a look of disbelief. He wants me to clean this up with the only shirt that I had. When René sees how upset this makes me, he just laughs harder.

I shake my head and pull the shirt up over my head. I'm not wearing a bra, so my tits are completely bare.

"Fuck, René, what can I give you for this one? I want to bite one of those nipples off." One of the other guests says and I see him lean back to brazenly palm his cock.

"Nah, this one isn't for sale. I told my boy that I was going to give him something special for his birthday and this pure piece of ass is something that I'm sure he will love." René picks up his cigar and takes a long toke.

"Pure?" the man says.

"A hundred percent certified virgin."

"Fuck! I need that shit." One of his guests stands up from his seat, a feral crazed look in his eyes.

"Uhn un." René catches his guest's attention, "This one is off limits. If I find out that anyone fucks with her, I'll make sure you don't see the next dawn. Leave her alone. Look, but don't touch."

"Oh man, you always save the best for yourself." One of the men whines and looks away from me.

"That's because I'm the boss." René laughs as I continue to clean up the mess the best that I can. At least I know that I don't have to worry about that. Still, I don't want to relax in this knowledge. Despite that I can't help but sigh a little breath of relief.

Another two days pass by, the beatings are becoming constant and the humiliations even more frequent. I'm starting to pray for the day to come that I will be able to go to Thomas, whatever he has planned for me has to be better than what his father is doing. It has to be.

I am working to clean up one of the back rooms that René has demanded to be spic and span before we are on our way. I don't necessarily mind the cleaning, it's the cleaning naked part that really bothers me.

"Damn girl, you sexy as fuck!"

I startle and turn in the direction of where the voice came from. There is a man leaning on the open door with a smoke between his lips as his eyes roam over my naked body. Just the feel of him looking at me has my skin breaking out in goosebumps.

"What do you want? I'm working." I try to make my voice sound strong, but instead it just sounds like I'm scared. I really am though.

"Oh, don't be like that baby. I just wanted to come talk to you for a few seconds. I know you got a bum deal out of this. You don't want to talk to me." The man slinks his way off the door and makes sure to close it behind him. I want to run out and scream. Only I know that no matter how fast I run there is no way that I was going to be able to make it past him. I would have to knock him down before I would be able to get through the door behind him.

"No, I can't talk right now. There is too much for me to get done. René will be here any minute and he is going to want to know why I haven't finished my chores. Please leave." I keep my voice as polite as I can muster and he just simply smirks.

"Oh no baby, I think that you can take a few minutes to talk to me. I can make you feel so very good." His strides are longer, I have to take a few steps back to make sure that he isn't right on top of me. I move back until I am flush against the wall and there is nowhere else for me to go. He smiles even wider when he realizes that I'm stuck.

"You're starting to hurt my feelings little girl. I just want to be your friend."

"I'm not a fucking little girl and I don't need any friends. If you want to help me than you will leave and let me do what I need to do in order to get this shit done. Back the hell off me!" I clench my fist. I wouldn't be able to knock him out, but I can tell from where I'm standing that his chin is weak. I can at least daze him. That is if I get enough space between me and him. I need to put all my weight into the swing. Except with being pressed up against the wall I can't do that.

"Back the hell off? Or what? What are you going to do if I don't? Tell me are you going to scream for daddy? Go ahead. He isn't here to help you. He will never be here again. We made sure of it." He starts to laugh, but my brain is misfiring with all the information that he just gave me. I can't understand what he is saying. What the fuck does he mean? What does he mean that my father will never be here again? Is he dead? Did they kill him?

"No! Fuck you!" I pull my hand back as far as I can and swing with all my might. I didn't have a lot of space, but the blow is hard enough that the bastard does fall down. I hop over his body and run for the door. Before my hand comes in contact with the knob, he is grabbing me from behind and swinging me back into the room.

"You stupid cunt! I was just trying to be nice to you and here you go making shit even worse for you." he snarls at me.

I stumble onto my ass and crab crawl away from him. "Leave me alone. You have to leave me alone."

"I don't have to do shit. No one fucking owns me." The man growls at me. He drops down to grab my foot, pulling me so that I am underneath him. I try to kick his hand away. I'm successful the first two times, but he eventually gets me still. When he starts to run one of his hands over the top of my chest, I know exactly what he is trying to do.

"You can't, René already told everyone that I was off limits."

"Oh no baby, he said that tight cunt of yours was off limits. He didn't say anything about anywhere else." He flips me over so that my face is pressed into the floor along with the other parts of the front of my body.

"No! Get off me!" My heart hammers against my chest and a cold sweat breaks out across my skin as I do my very best to buck him off of me. The fact that I'm already naked means that he doesn't really have to work too hard to get to what he wants.

"Fuck yes, keep fighting bitch ... I love that shit." he grunts and I hear the clinking of his belt buckle as he yanks it off.

"Stop!" I scream, but he has my face smashed down so hard into the ground that I can't really get my mouth to open all the way up. "Please get the fuck off of me. Stop it!" I cry out and try again to push him away.

"Oh fuck, I'm going to fucking destroy you." He kneels up and I can feel his disgusting dick bobbing up and down against my ass cheeks.

"No, please. Please." I beg, but I'm so out of breath that I don't have any more strength to fight. I just lay there trying to make sure that I don't pass out.

I clench up the best that I can—my last line of defense.

"Open up slut. Don't make this any fucking harder than it's already going to be." He presses against me, but he isn't able to penetrate.

I hear a soft click and then a loud blast right above my head. I scream out in shock and my eyes slam shut. Suddenly I feel rain, but instead of small droplets I feel big globs of something falling all over me. When I open my eyes again, I can see that the rain that I'm feeling is actually blood and the big chunks are tissue, actually brains.

"What the fuck!" I start to panic when I turn around and can see the man still kneeling above me. His body stuck in that final stance even though there is a huge gaping hole in his head where his right eye used to be. I pull myself up and try to crawl away, but that one motion is enough to have his body fall right down on top of me.

"Ahh, get him off. Oh shit." I push at him, but my hands slip in the mess that is his blood and flesh. I'm screaming as it feels like I'm never going to be able to move this big man.

"Shut up with all that shit. He's not going to do anything to you. Just roll him off." I hear René above me, but he doesn't bend down to help me at all. In fact, he sounds as if I'm a nuisance to him. I follow his directions though. I roll and the man tumbles off of me.

"Thank you." I mumble out, if he hadn't come along this could have be a whole lot worse.

"Girl don't thank me. I could give two shits what anyone does to you or those little holes you got, but I told him you were off limits. He should have fucking listened to me." He shrugs and drops a bag in the corner away from the blood. "Besides I'm sure whatever my son has planned for you tonight will trump anything that this bastard had planned. From what I've been told my son isn't the nicest when it comes to the ladies."

I sit up and stare at him, knowing that I won't find even a speck of compassion. Although I hoped that maybe I would find some indifference. I don't, but he is getting a kick out of tormenting me. This shit is actually bringing him pleasure.

"Get this shit and yourself cleaned up. Then get dressed. It's Thomas' birthday, finally you are going to be out of my hair." He waves his hand absent-mindedly and turns to leave the room. I sit there with the dead body, blood and flesh all over my hair and skin, and brand new clothes in a bag off to the side. I'm not going to make it out of this. If what Thomas has planned for me is worse than this, I won't survive.

CHAPTER

CELINE

The dress that René gave me is too fucking short for me to do anything besides sit. I cross my legs at the ankle to try and keep some type of modesty, but if I move forward too far everyone is going to get a full show.

"Don't let her out of your sight." René says as he walks over to the other side of the large ferry. I didn't know where the party was actually taking place. Though it must be a big deal, because there were so many people on the boat. Some of the people I knew from the boxing circuit and others I knew from seeing their faces on the TV and news. René had all matter of guests on this ferry, from criminal to the elite. I'm positive that not one of them would go against him. He commands that much loyalty. I'm sure if he killed me right now, none of them would even bat an eyelash.

I look around and try to see if I can find Thomas anywhere. Only he isn't on the ferry, it must be taking us to the actual location of the party. I'm still the big surprise.

"You are going to be Thomas' new pet?" One of the guards stands in front of me.

"What?" I don't look up into his face. I can basically hear the antagonistic look on his face.

"That's such a shame. You are a pretty one. By the time he is finished with you, no one is going to want you anymore. He takes his time breaking the women that his father brings to him. He's angry and takes it out on the women his father force feeds him."

31

Now I have to look up to see what the hell he is talking about. Thomas has always had a thing for me. At least I thought he did. He seemed more intrigued with me as a person than necessarily trying to get with me though.

"What the hell is that supposed to mean?" I ask, but make sure to keep my voice down. I don't want anyone else to get in on this conversation.

"Oh, we all think Tommy boy is lying to himself. We think he is more of a catcher than an actual pitcher, if you know what I mean. I just don't think he is ready to admit that to himself. His father sees it, but he just can't stand to have one of his sons be like that." The guard shrugs like either way it doesn't bother him.

Like what? I think back on all the interactions that I have ever had with Thomas. It did seem like he was a little softer and I was always able to intimidate him. I've never been scared of Thomas either. In fact, it always felt like I was more dominant than him. Not that being soft is criteria for being gay, but maybe he was so attracted to me because he found my aggressiveness attractive.

"You think he is gay?" I whisper and look around, again making sure that no one hears me, but the guard in front of me.

"Oh yeah, for sure. He won't admit it though, his father either. So, René keeps throwing women at him. Expects him to fall for one of them or at least get one of them knocked up when all the boy does is go into a rage and brutalizes them. The last girl he bit her clit clean off, because she couldn't make him come. Like it was her fault he wasn't attracted to her as he thought he should be. He's a big fan of sodomy though. One of the girls will have a colostomy bag for the rest of her life. Yeah, he's going to fuck you up real good." He cackles as he takes a few steps away from me.

I wasn't being gifted to Thomas, because he had a thing for me. I was being gifted to him, so he had another woman to torture, because of his own confusion. I don't know why I'd ever thought that I would be able to go through with this. I pray that my father can forgive me for what I'm about to do. I have to get out of here and right now on this ferry may be the only time that I have the chance to do that.

The guards that are supposed to be watching me both have their backs to me. They are watching the crowd all the while making sure that I don't move. It's true in order for me to get off the boat I would have to go right through them, but only if I planned to get off the boat the traditional and safe way. I don't.

I lean back over the railing and can see that the fall to the water is not that far. At least I don't think it is. The water itself is murky and it's dark out already. I can only see the reflection of a few lights shining on the water. The port is far away, but there is shoreline close by. I've always been a good swimmer and positive that I can make it. If I can't at least I'll only drown and not actually be tortured to death. I will take drowning over Thomas any day.

I wait until all the talking on board gets louder in volume and the guards move a little further away. As softly as I possibly can, slip over the rail and jump into the water. It was much simpler than I would have thought minus the fact that my hands were tied together. They were bound in front of me, but I knew how to swim without moving my hands. I could use my legs and the dolphin kick to get me where I needed to go. It was my only option until I was able to get these ties off.

"Holy shit!" I hear someone scream out as my body hits the water.

"Motherfucker!" screams another person and then I hear shots hit the water. I quickly move into action and begin to swim with everything I have. I hadn't practiced the dolphin kick technique in quite some time. It takes a bit more effort out of me than I want, but I do it. Soon the bullets stop flying and when I look I can see that the boat is no longer moving forward. They are going to come in the water for me. I have no time to rest, I have to keep going. I push myself as hard as I can go. I kick and kick for what feels like eternity. My eyes and nose burn from the filthy water getting into them. It feels as if my lungs might explode from the constant deep breaths that I am having to take to continue swimming. I feel my legs trying to cramp up, but I fight through the pain. I don't have time to be in pain right now. They are going to find me and when they do, I know that my punishment is going to be much worse. I don't see a dinghy in the water, but I do see a light shining back and forth. I laugh softly in disbelief. Somehow, they can't see me. It's so dark that they have no idea which direction I have gone.

The shore is right there. A small foot bridge looms over head and though I don't hear any traffic I know that something has to still be open. This is New Orleans, no matter the time of night there is always something open.

I stop for only a second. It's the wrong fucking thing to do, the moment I let my legs relax cramping takes hold. I try to stretch my legs out, but I can't. I slap at the water desperately, but my hands are still tied. I'm going to fucking drown right as I got away.

CHAPTER

8

JAMESON

"Jam, I need you to go check on Capri. There were a few assholes that thought it was a good idea to harass her on her way home last night." Archer tells me. It's close to three in the morning. Normal people would be sleeping at this time. "Unless you want to knock out, but you usually want to ride after Monica shows up."

I roll my eyes. Was everyone in my business when it came to Monica? I couldn't be mad about it though. It's not like she was quiet about how bad she wanted me back. These fights between me and her were becoming more and more frequent. Besides, Archer was right. I was agitated not only from this shit with the counterfeiter, but with her as well.

"Nah, I'm good. I'll go check on her." Capri is Pirate's little sister. She tries her best to stay out of our life. She claims it's too gory for her, but she knows when to call her big brother's angry biker friends to intimidate the hell out of someone. The woman isn't stupid.

I pick up my keys and my lid only stopping to check on Shyne. He is busy testing Finn, our newest prospect. Finn's only been out of active duty for about six months so there is a lot that he has to learn. The kid is only 21 years old, all baby faced and wide eyes. His mother let him sign up for the Navy when he was 17, one tour was enough for him.

"How is it going in here?" I stick my head in and watch Finn cleaning up the empty bullet casings that Shyne has thrown onto the ground. He has him doing that shit blind folded too. Why the fuck is he doing it? I have no idea, but I'm not going to question it. Besides

35

Finn had already checked out, but of course we did feel the need to haze him for a while. Being a prospect basically meant that you were our bitch. If you wanted to be a fucking Wing, then you would do what the fuck you had to do in order to become one. If that meant you would roll around on the floor with shell casings in your fucking underwear than that is what you would do.

"Good, Finn makes a good pup." Shyne pushes Finn forward, but he doesn't fall forward. He just turns and I can see his jaw clenching with something to say.

He wasn't used to taking shit. That is what I want to see, we didn't need anyone who was too pussy to stand up for themselves. Sure, they were expected to do what we asked them to do as prospects. Despite that, if they were too willing to get beat down with no talk back, we didn't really want them.

"Keep it up Finn, we will make a Wing out of you yet." I turn and close the door behind me shaking my head at the ridiculousness of it. Finn would be there all night.

I pass Yang on the way to my bike and let him know that I'm on my way to check on Capri.

"You need any back up. I can get one of the prospects to come keep watch."

"No, I'm good. I need to clear my fucking mind anyway." I shake my head and get on my Softail. If there is anything in this world that I love more than my own fucking life, then it would be this fucking bike. When I finally got home to the states the first thing I did before even checking on Monica and the house was to make sure that my bike was still safely parked away in the garage. I should have stayed there a few more minutes and maybe I wouldn't have caught my wife playing hide the salami with the grocer.

Just thinking about it is enough to get my blood boiling again.

"Yeah, I feel you brother." Yang backs off, "Do what you have to do."

I don't even respond, just take off straight towards Capri's place. The wind and the solitude are something I have grown addicted to. My brothers keep me grounded, but it's this solitude that keeps me sane. Honestly, it feels like when everything else is going to shit that this is the only time that I can just let my mind free.

It doesn't take very long for me to get to Capri's. I park my bike and walk into the bar.

"Hey baby, you know you didn't have to come. They know better than to mess with me after the beating Shyne put on them yesterday." Capri calls out as she rushes to put the bottles of alcohol back where they belong.

"Aw, darling you know it's no trouble. None at all." I settle on one of the stools and watch her work. "You need any help over there?" I realize she is lifting a lot of heavy boxes. Though I know she is more than capable, I don't feel too easy about letting her do that shit by herself. My momma had raised me to be something of a gentleman.

Before she could even answer, I walk over to the other side of the bar and began to lift the rest of the boxes for her. She shouldn't have to do all that work on her own.

"Jameson, you're too good to me." Capri lets out a deep breath. She relaxes against the bar for a second while I go ahead and put the merchandise where it belongs.

Once I finish with that chore, I make sure to walk around the area and put all the chairs on the tables so she wouldn't have to lift those either. All of it doing a very poor job at keeping my mind off of Monica. What the fuck gives her the right to try and force her way back into my fucking life after the shit that she's pulled.

"You know if you slam those chairs down any harder, I'm sure you going to break every last one of them." Capri says from where she is standing looking at me.

I shake myself out of my thoughts only to realize that I'd been slamming the chairs down on the tables too aggressively.

"Sorry about that sweetheart." I shoot her a soft smile, but my eyes stay on hers as she is still staring at me.

"Something interesting about me?"

"Fuck yes. there is something interesting about you. When you going to let me get on that ride Jameson?" Capri let's her tongue stick out between her teeth as her eyes continue to rake over my body.

"Oh darling, you know we can't do that." I reply and come closer to where she is. She bridges the gap to press a hand to my chest under my kutte, letting her fingers trail over my pecs and down over my abs.

Her hand drops all the way down to my dick that has already begun to harden in my pants. "Oh, I think your body thinks we can do that."

I put my hand over hers and press up into her palm once before I move her hand away and bring it up to my mouth. "I never said I wasn't capable or even that I didn't fucking want to. I said we can't." I kiss her palm hoping to soften the blow. With her being Pirate's little sister, she was off limits to the rest of us. Pirate might have been older than all of us, but he could still kick some ass. "Pirate would fuck me up if I even touched one hair on your head."

"I'm completely hairless, in all the places that count, actually." She smirks at me before she backs up to turn and put the rest of what she needs to away.

I groan as I imagine what her bare pussy actually looks like. Fuck if I wasn't so sure Pirate would have my ass, I would take her up on the offer. Capri is gorgeous. Her hair is long and black with a permanent wave to it while her lips are pouty and look soft as fuck. My cock would fit perfectly between them

I shake the thoughts out of my mind and try to think of something else. There is nothing that I can do about Capri. I don't need any problems with my brother.

"You good girl? It's time for me to get back to bed." I yell and she hustles out from the back.

"Yeah, I'm good Jameson. Let's go."

I follow behind her car on my bike as she makes her way to her house. I'm sure that the bastards won't be back over here to mess with her, but I really don't want to leave any chances.

She walks into her house and then raises her hand to give me a wave. I nod to her and then turn to leave. I know she's safe now so I can get back home and get some sleep. I'm not as relaxed as I want to be and part of me thinks that maybe I should have taken her up on her offer to get a little release. Hell, Pirate would never know.

I shake my head and get that stupid thought out of it. I know no matter how fucking desperate I become I'm never going to go against one of my brothers. Pirate said she was off limits so she's fucking off limits.

I throttle my bike up and feel the wind whipping against my face. A loud pop causes me to swerve and look behind me.

"What the fuck!" My breathing is becoming erratic as I search for the threat. The noise sounds again and I realize it's just someone's fucked up car back firing. No one is shooting at me. There is no one out here to get me.

I pull over to the side of the road to get myself under control, but the images in my head have already started.

They say when you come back from war there are things that you leave behind and there are things that you bring home. This shit I really wish I would have left behind. Even just that small sound is enough to transport me back to all the fucked up places where we had to worry about who was shooting at us and if there was going to be an enemy around the corner. Hell, one of the main reasons I felt so at ease with the Wings of Diablo was because there was so much that reminded me of my deployment. Though the brotherhood was the best part. I knew any one of those men in my club would give their life for me. They would jump on a grenade if it meant that I would be able to get out alive and I would do the same for them. It's when I'm alone that I don't fare so well. I know I'm on edge, because of the shit that went down with Monica. Most of the time a ride is all that I need to clear my head, but it seems like today it just isn't enough.

I park my bike on the side of the road and get off to walk towards the foot bridge. Maybe a little meditation will be enough to get me out of this fucking funk. I put my hands on the rail and look into the deep dirty water. It wasn't the prettiest fucking picture, but it looked peaceful.

There is a ferry on the other side of the river, but it looks like it has stopped. I vaguely wonder if it's in distress, but I don't see anything abnormal about it. Even if it is, there is nothing that I can do about it anyway. I take a few steadying breaths and look back to the water. I had to get my shit together. My head jerks to the side as I see something splash down by the bank. What the hell kind of fish makes that big of a splash? I scan the area and try to see if I can see anything, maybe it's a fucking gator. I've seen stranger shit before.

At first, I don't see anything, but then all of a sudden a pair of alabaster arms shoot out of the surface of water followed by a head gasping for air before it sinks back under the water.

"Oh shit! Oh shit, hold on!" I yell and take off like a bat out of hell. I race down the small hill towards the water. I kick off my boots and take care to throw my kutte on top of them before I jump into the water in the direction that I saw the person. I dive under the water, but I can't see shit with it being so dark and with all the silt.

I pop back up to the surface and scan the area quickly, "Fuck. What the shit!" I swirl back in the opposite direction and a head pops back up in my view. I dart over there as fast as I can and just as the person goes back under the water I grab onto their arm and tug them back up.

"Hold on. I fucking got you. Just hold the fuck on." I grunt out. I swim back towards the embankment, but it seems like the person is fighting against my hold. "Fucking relax, I got you."

I pull the person out of the water, and fall down myself trying to catch my breath. I turn to the side and see legs—long toned wet legs.

"Hey, you ok?" I bark out as I try to grab the woman to turn her over. Her head pops up and she rolls to her back pushing away from me with one of her legs. It's only then that I see her hands are actually tied together. She is in a skin tight black dress and no shoes, looking like she just escaped a stretch in prison. What the fuck had happened to her?

"Oh shit, hold up. Let me help you. Let me get this off you." I reach out for her hands, "I'll get you back there."

"No! I'm not going back!" She swings her arms in my direction and her elbow connects perfectly with my nose. Lights flash in my eyes as they water. I squeeze my nose with my hand.

"Fuck!" I roar in pain and hear her scrambling up the side of the hill. I open my eyes and get a full view of her ass as she scrabbles her way up and over the rail.

I try to pull myself up, but the blow to my face left me dizzy and out of sorts. She had hit me in a perfect spot, there is no doubt in my head that she is trained. She has to be.

I slowly make my way up the side of the hill, blood dripping from my nose and sliding down the back of my throat. I hack it up and spit on the side of the hill before I make my way to the solid ground of the foot bridge. I look from left to right, but I don't see her anywhere. She couldn't have gotten far. There is no way that I'm just going to leave her there for someone to hurt her even worse than she has already been hurt.

I race over to my bike, sniffing a few times as the blood trickling from my nose begins to slow down. I jump on my beast, throw on my lid, and hit the mounted phone piece that is on my bike that rings directly to the club. I wait as the line trills in the Bluetooth receiver embedded in my helmet. "Wings." It's Yang, he is probably the only one who is up right now watching over everything.

"Brother, it's Jameson. I need y'all to be on alert. I'm bringing someone in." At least I think I'm bringing someone in. If I can fucking find her that is.

"You need back up? Is it Capri?"

I can hear the panic start to build in his voice.

"No, no back up yet and not Capri. Ya'll ain't going to believe this shit ... I'll explain when I get home. Just stay on alert and by the phone in case anything changes." I give the order and hang up before he has anything else to say. I know he's going to be busy waking everyone up.

I roll slowly making sure to check in every fucking alley and in every fucking storefront, but I don't see her. Finally, I see something moving in one of the side alleys about a quarter of a mile away from where I had found her. Someone is trying to break into the small coffee shop. I hop off my bike and rush to the alley.

"Hey wait a minute." I call out

"No, please." The woman takes off in the opposite direction. I follow her and quickly catch up to her. This alley is a dead end and there is nowhere for her to go, not that she doesn't try. When she gets to the end, I hear her whimper and then she tries to climb up the chain-link fence even though her hands are still tied together. She doesn't get very far. I am able to grab her by the waist and pull her down.

"No, no, let me go." She squirms and still tries to get away.

"Fucking hell woman, calm down. I'm not trying to hurt you." I fight with her, but still try to keep myself from roughing her up. What-ever she has been through obviously has her fighting to survive right now.

"Sure you're not, you're just trying to take me back to Thomas. I'm not fucking going." She curses me and falls back into a fighting stance. Even with her hands tied I can tell she isn't just going to let me throw her over my shoulder and take her.

I stand back and put my hands up so that she can see that I'm not trying to threaten her. "Look lady, I don't know who the fuck Thomas is. I'm not going to take you anywhere you don't want to go, but you almost nearly fucking drowned. Your limping like your leg is messed up, your hands are tied together and you're fucking barefoot. I just want to fucking help you."

She doesn't back down, but she doesn't charge me or anything like that. I pull out my knife and show it to her which causes her to jump back slightly.

"For the binding on your wrists. I can't break them with my hands, but I can cut them off. Let me cut you free." I say and take a step in her direction.

Her eyes follow the knife as I move over to where she is. It takes a few minutes to cut through the ties, but I can see she still is a bit edgy. I put the knife back in my pocket and slowly back away from her.

"Just leave me alone. Let me go." She whimpers as she tries to move even further back.

"No, I'm not going to leave you alone right now darling. It seems as if you need a bit of help. I don't know what the fuck is going on, but I'm not going to leave you alone. Just let me help you." I take a few steps in her direction.

"You don't know him?" She asks softly.

I may know exactly who she is talking about, but she isn't really being specific, "No. I don't know him. I'm just around here checking on a friend when I saw you. Come on babe, let me help you." I reach my hand out.

"Don't fucking call me babe, you don't know me." She snaps at me.

My lips twist up slightly, she's a firecracker. "Sorry, about that, what would you have me call you then?"

"I'm Celine, my name is Celine." She grabs my hand and I pull her closer to me.

"Jameson." My voice is nothing more than a whisper.

"You're really going to help me?" She asks and I can see that her eyes are beginning to water.

"I'm going to do the best that I can."

She basically falls into me and starts to cry. I don't know what the hell is happening with this woman, but I know that she isn't in a good way. I have to help her.

CHAPTER 9

JAMESON

The ride back to the club house is slower than I would have liked, but Celine kept whipping her head around to look for the people that she said were after her. I have to help her keep her legs in the right position but even just glancing at them I can see they are cramping. I knew she was in pain but I needed to stay balanced. I didn't want to chance having the bike tip over, because she was moving around too much back there.

I pull up to the clubhouse and I can feel the grip that she has on me getting tighter.

"What the hell is this place?" She hisses in my ear when I pull the bike to a stop.

"This is my home and the clubhouse for the Wings of Diablo MC."

"What the hell is that? Are you in some type of gang or something … because a fucking gang isn't going to help me right now."

"It's not a gang, Celine." I roll my eyes. I'm so fucking tired of having people constantly think that just because we wore the same shit and all lived together it was a fucking gang. For fuck's sake, do they call the people in the military a fucking gang? "We're a brotherhood."

"Yeah, really looks like ya'll sit around at night and sing kumbaya." She slowly dismounts the bike, rubbing at her cramped up thighs and does her best to warm up herself up. Dresses are not ideal for riding on the back of a motorcycle.

"Do you want the fucking help? Or are you just going to stand there and judge shit you obviously know nothing about?" I slam my lid onto the handlebars and make sure my bike is secure before I raise off it.

"I'm sorry, you're right I shouldn't be judging … I'm sorry." She looks me in the eyes and it feels like all the fucking annoyance that I had just felt was gone. I let out a breath and examine her closely. She is wet, dirty, and a complete mess. Though, fuck me if she isn't one of the most gorgeous women I have ever fucking seen. Her legs and arms are muscular, like she has been lifting weights, but she still has a bit of softness to her. Her hair is long and from what I can tell I think it might be a dark blonde or light brown, with it being wet I really can't say. It's her eyes though that capture my attention. They are a normal blue color, but it's almost as if I can see the fire burning inside them. I can tell that she is a fighter—strong and never quitting.

"Fine, let's go." I don't have time to gawk at her the way that I want to. I need to get her in to see Archer. We all need to know exactly what the fuck we are dealing with right now.

She crosses her hands over her chest trying to get some warmth. I realize that I haven't told her what to expect. It's obvious she's never been in this situation before and the last thing I want for her to do is to go in there and try to lie to Archer. He'll be able to sniff that shit out and we wouldn't be able to help her.

"Listen to me. When we get in there you have to tell Archer everything. Don't leave anything out and don't lie."

She stops and squints her eyes at me as if she can't understand what the hell I'm talking about. "I don't have to do shit. I don't *have* to tell him anything more than I think I should. That isn't the fucking deal."

"No? Then what is the fucking deal? You need me to drive you back down to the fucking riverbank so you can swim the fuck back or do you want help?"

"Fuck you!" She growls at me and instead of backing up she widens her stance. This girl is ready to fight me. "I don't need your fucking pity. I don't owe you shit. You said you would help me. I didn't know there were fucking stipulations."

I hear the door open to the clubhouse and I expect to see Yang, but instead I see Pirate. It must be his turn to take over watch.

"Hey, what the fuck is this?" He asks moving in closer to her.

"Get away from me." Celine tries to take a step back, but Pirate takes another one forward.

"I don't have to do nothing little lady. Bring your ass in here."

I throw my hand out the very second that I see Pirate try to grab her. I didn't know much about Celine, but I know she isn't someone to fucking play with. She doesn't like to be grabbed.

She takes one steadying step back and raises her hands up in perfect formation. Directly in front of her face, fists balled up and ready to fucking fly.

"What the fuck is this bullshit? Little girl, you don't know what the fuck you are doing."

"Pirate, don't" I bark out at him in warning, but it's too late.

He reaches out to grab her again and she lets her fists fly perfectly.

2-1-2, cross-jab-cross

Pirate's face snaps back in three quick successions and he falls straight back to the ground.

My mouth drops into a wide O and I have to bite my lips so I don't burst out laughing. She just knocked him the fuck out.

He shook his head for a second before he rolled over and tried to get up. "You fucking bitch, I'll kill you. I swear to God I will." He slurred out.

I stand in front of him so that he can't charge her. "Bro, you good?" I'm still trying not to laugh, but I can't help it. That shit was more than perfect.

"Fuck that bitch."

"You tried to grab her; she was just protecting herself."

"She punched me in the goddamn face."

"Several times too." I say and that is all it takes. I bend over and start laughing like a mad man.

Pirate glares at me and rolls his eyes before he turns and storms back into the clubhouse.

"Pirate! Don't be mad! Everyone gets their ass whooped by a woman at least once in their life." I have to brace myself on my knees, so I don't fall down to the ground and laugh until my fucking eyes water.

46

When I turn back to Celine, I can see she is still ready to fight, but she is smiling hard too.

"Hey, what the fuck is this shit?" Archer sticks his head out the door and I stop laughing immediately. "Get the fuck in here so we can get this shit over with."

That was an order and like any good solider, I follow my fucking orders.

"Let's go." I get myself together and reach out for Celine.

"Who is that?" She asks, following close behind me.

"Archer, he is our leader. The president of the club. Remember what I told you out front. Tell him the truth. He will help you and keep you safe, but if you lie to him … he will send you on your way."

"Fine, I'll be honest." She moves further into my back. This badass woman who had just knocked out a grown ass man is holding herself against me like I'm her savior. It's a strange fucking feeling.

We walk inside the building and I swear I feel her tremble behind me.

"Picking up strays I see." Shyne says from where he is sitting.

I hold her back not wanting her to say anything to Shyne. He could be a dick sometimes, but he was a good man. Besides I was already going to have to explain what the hell had happened to Pirate. That bridge was one more light from being burned.

"What the hell is going on with this?" Archer asks, but doesn't move to look at the girl behind me.

"I don't know all the specifics yet. I went to check on Capri and on my way back I found this one drowning in the fucking river."

"Drowning? What the fuck was she doing in the damn river, dressed like that?" Yang leaned over to the side and tried to examine the woman behind me. She just moved further behind me. She didn't fight like a skittish woman, in fact she fought like a fucking wildcat.

"I don't know brother. In fact the most that I've been able to get out of her so far is that she doesn't want me to send her back and she is running away from someone. I'm assuming that someone was on the ferry that she jumped off with her hands still tied together."

"She was bound?" Archer is more intrigued now. Back when he was with the main chapter of WOD, they had a huge problem with sex trafficking. The last thing he wants to hear about is women being kidnapped.

I nod my head and try to move so that she is in his sight. Just as I do the door opens and Pirate walks in still wiping the blood from his mouth.

"What the fuck happened to you?" Yang asks.

"This broad punched me in the face." He grumbles gesturing with his head towards Celine.

"No, she knocked you the fuck out." I chuckle, trying to lighten the mood.

"Is that why your ass was laid out on the ground out there? Fuck, I thought you were playing or some shit." Archer shook his head from side to side, shame and disbelief on his face.

"I just wasn't expecting it." Pirate retorts.

"The first one you weren't expecting, what do you have to say about the other two?" Celine says from behind me. Her head poked out, eyes glaring at Pirate.

"She chin checked you, bro?" Shyne began to cackle.

"Gotta teach these boys how to bob and weave." Celine plays right along.

"Fuck this shit." Pirate storms off clearly not happy with being the butt of the joke.

"Hold up! We still got business to handle, leave your hurt pride out there on the ground." Archer said from where he was standing before he turns his gaze back on Celine, "You want to tell me what the hell is going on and what you were doing in the fucking river with your hands tied together?"

"I had to get away from Thomas." She spoke clearly.

"Thomas your husband or something like that?"

"Fuck that, hell no. I have never had anything to do with him like that. I don't even like him. The problem is my father fucked up and now he owes a debt to someone who thinks they can force me to be with Thomas. If I don't go to Thomas, they may kill my father. René doesn't play around."

"René?" I ask and the hairs on the back of my neck stand up. She can't be talking about the same fucking René.

"You mean the bastard that runs the underground fighting ring, René?" Archer takes another step forward, suddenly more interested than before.

"Yeah, my father is a boxer. He is actually the champ of René's operation. René told him to take a dive and he was going to, but the opponent did before he could. The bet was me." She shrugs, but I can see that she is hurt. Her eyes are cast down and her shoulders are hunched forward.

"What the fuck? Why the hell would your pops bet some shit like that?"

Celine's eyes jump up to mine at my outburst. If her tongue could slither from her mouth like a fucking snake, I swear it did just then, "You don't know shit about what my father had to do. René doesn't really give people much of a choice when it comes to what they bet. Once you are deep enough into the shit you don't have a choice. My father tried to throw the fight in the manner that René demanded of him, but René had already told the other fighter to fall before he could. So, before you go judging my fucking father make sure you know all the fucking facts first."

I put my hands up again for the second time tonight to show her that I'm not the fucking threat. I was simply asking questions using the information that I had been given.

"So what were you doing on the ferry? Why are you dressed like this?" Archer continue looking for more answers.

"Today is Thomas, René's son's, birthday. I was supposed to be his birthday gift, except I learned this evening what he does with the women in his possession. The man is sadistic. I thought that I could handle whatever they threw at me so that I could get my father out of trouble. But after the week that I had stayed with René, I know that I can't. I'd die before I ever see my father again." A tear drops from her eye and she quickly blinks it away as if she thought it was a sign of weakness.

"Hey, you did what you had to do. There is no fucking shame in any of this. Did he tell your father that he would be able to get you back?" I ask wondering what could have persuaded him to let her go with a sleazeball like fucking René.

"Not in those exact words, but he did say that once Thomas got tired of me that I would be able to go back to my father. He made it seem like once he had his fill, I'd be free." She tightens her grip around her waist.

"He would have never gotten tired of you, in fact I'm not sure you would have ever seen the outside world again. You did the right thing jumping the fuck off that boat. What I'm trying to figure out is how a woman with your clear fighting skill was even taken in the first place." Pirate smirks, rubbing his jaw. I'm glad that there are no hard feelings.

"One on one, I don't have any doubt I could take him on, but with René there are always guards upon guards. I would knock out one of them and three more would jump me. Three on one is too much for anyone to take on."

"Huh, I hear that." Pirate kicks his feet up on the chair next to him and leans back on the back legs of his own chair.

"Well, you don't have to worry about no one not having your back now. You're with us, we're not going to just let someone come and take you." Archer nods his head once and starts to walk off. "Jameson, set her up in one of the guest rooms. Then get some shut eye. Bright and early get everyone up for church. We got some fucking business to handle." He doesn't turn around, but I know exactly what business he is talking about. René has got to go.

I usher Celine to one of the back rooms. We have quite a few available, because we don't let any of the club bunnies stay on the premises. Although we do get quite a few allies that come through for visits or to lay low. Hell, Wire was just here a few days ago. Poor man, losing everything like that. Same thing had happened to Prez and he wasn't ever the same man.

"You going to tie me up or some shit like that, because if that is what you are planning to do, I'll just be on my way."

My eyes scrunch in as I wait for her to finish the tirade that she is going on, "Darling, cool the fuck out. Just like I told you in that fucking alley, I'm not here to hurt you. I'm getting a little pissed off that you keep expecting me to."

"You're human, I don't have a lot of faith in mankind. They tend to only look out for themselves so if that is your plan just let me know so I can be on my way. I have to get my father."

I want to laugh, not that I found her to be funny, instead she was refreshing. For the most part the women that I'd found myself around were all very woe is me—especially Monica. Everything that was happening even if it was her fault was just another reason for someone to feel sorry for her. She thrived off fucking pity. Celine was the complete opposite. Her father had screwed her royally. The blame was completely on him. Instead of looking for pity which she could completely get, she was trying to find a way to get to her father. To find a way for them both to come out of this shit intact. Her strength was refreshing and attractive as fuck.

"I agree with your sentiment on mankind, but I can only swear to you that we aren't here to screw you over. Haven't you ever heard the saying, 'the enemy of my enemy is my friend?' We might be fighting René for different shit, but we both want him gone." I explain to her.

"You think your crew is big enough to take down René? Do you realize how deep into this community he is?"

"I'm not saying it won't be a fucking fight, but we don't quit."

"Hmm, sometimes you have to know when to throw in the towel." She turns away from me and looks around the room. "You guys are going to let me stay here?"

"Yeah. You are free to stay here for as long as you need until we get this shit handled or you can go back to your father."

"Tomorrow morning I'll go back."

I didn't think that was the best idea. I'm sure that's the first place that René looked for her after he realized that she was no longer on the Ferry is her father's house. Unfortunately, I wouldn't be surprised if he had killed her father already.

"Sure. Tomorrow then."

She shuffles from foot to foot like she wants to say something, so I don't move.

"No one is going to try and mess with me ... I can sleep?" Her eyes dart over to the freshly made bed and then back to the floor.

I don't know what the fuck that René bastard did to her, but if I could rip his fucking arms from his body right now I would. The cowardly piece of shit.

"No one will fuck with you. You have my fucking word. In fact, my bedroom is on the other side of this wall." I point to the wall that her bed is pressed up against. "If something happens or someone even knocks on your door, you come get me. Nothing is too small, you understand?" I stare at her for a second before I nod and turn to walk out the room. I didn't need to wait for her to thank me. I knew she was grateful from the way her shoulders dropped, as if a small weight had been lifted off.

I make my way to my room next door and pull out a shirt with some compression tights. I'm sure none of it would fit her, but it is something that she would be able to wear while she is waiting. I pulled a pair of socks out as well. This should be enough to keep her warm for at least tonight. I didn't have a hair dryer or anything like that, but I hope a towel will be enough for her. I pull one of those out of the side linen closet and drape it over my shoulder.

I walk out of my room and open the door to hers.

"What the fuck! Get out!" She screams, trying to cover her naked body with her arms.

Oh shit!

I turn around as fast as possible, "Fuck, I'm sorry. I should have knocked. I'm sorry. That wasn't intentional." I had just spent the past few minutes trying to convince her that no one was going to mess with her and here I am basically a glorified peeping tom.

"What are you doing in here?" She asks and though I can't see her, I hear her voice coming in fast. She's pissed and she should be. I'm not. It may not have happened in the most honorable fashion, but even that quick microsecond I was able to catch a glimpse of her. Her body is what most of my fucking wet dreams are made of. It's clear that she is in good shape, her stomach is flat and toned. I can see the outline of her abs, but they're not severe. Her breasts look firm from what I could see and her pussy. That kitty is bare and ready for me to feast on it.

Fuck! I look down and in just that small amount of time that I reminisce on her is enough to have me aching with a raging hard on. Shit I had to get this shit under control fast or she would think that I was a complete creeper. I didn't really need her to trust me, but I wanted her to.

"I just came to give you some clothes, I should have knocked. I'm sorry." This is more apologizing than I am used to doing.

I bunch the clothes and towel in one hand to put it out to the side so that she can take it from me and I don't have to turn around. There was no way my cock was going down any time soon. I'd just have to hide it.

She snatches the clothing from my hand. I expect her to push me out, but instead I hear skin pushing through fabric.

"Thank you." Her tone is softer, more relaxed.

"You're welcome. I have a meeting in the morning, so I'll be heading to my bunk. If you need anything just knock on the wall." I say over my shoulder still not wanting to turn around and see her in a state of undress.

"I think I might just burst in." She quips.

I know she means the door, but I'm thinking about ramming myself into something completely different.

I groan and walk away without taking another peek at her. I don't need any more images of her to keep me up tonight.

CHAPTER 10

JAMESON

"Get your fucking head down!" I yell at the new recruit that just got transferred into my unit. I bet when he signed up and finished his basic fucking training that he wasn't expecting to be shipped off into a fucking fire fight his first tour. Those are the breaks.

"Get down now!" I yell at him again as bullet upon bullet whizzes in the air right above my head.

"What the fuck! What the fuck is going on?" Shyne calls out from where he is lying next to me. This was supposed to be a quick patrol. No one should be here. Yet, my whole fucking unit is pinned down in a ditch with at least a dozen enemies firing at us.

"Keep your shit together." I press myself harder into the dirt.

"I have to get out of here! I don't belong here!" The newbie cries out and I see him crawl out of cover as if he were going to be able to run out of danger.

"No! Get down! Stop!"

He's only 19, just a fucking kid.

I dig my fingers in the dirt as I watch him jump out of cover and a flurry of bullets burst through his body. A spray of red mists the air as the boy's body leans back slightly before he falls down to his knees and another bullet explodes through his head.

"No!" I hear myself roaring and I can feel Shyne pulling me back to keep in cover.

There is nothing that I can do. Nothing that anyone can do, but they are still peppering his dead body with bullets. Why are they doing that? He's dead already.

"Stop! Stop it!" I scream wanting nothing more than to pull my brother out of there.

"Fuck, they're coming. Jam, what do we do?" Randy grabs my gear and gives me a shake. The enemy is closing in around us, what the fuck are we going to do?

The world turns black as hands come towards me from every fucking angle. I fight them off the best that I can, but I can't win. Grunts and moans from my brothers hit my ears like they are in surround sound, but I can't get to them. It feels like someone is trying to drown me.

"Jameson!"

My eyes pop open and my heart is beating double time in my chest. Sweat from my brow drips into my eyes and I have to blink a few times to clear my vision.

It was a dream, just a fucking dream.

I exhale a few times and take note of where I am. I'm on the floor of my room and there is something under me.

I lift up slightly. "Fuck! Celine!" I rise up to my knees, but she doesn't move.

I still have my hand wrapped around her neck. I let go slowly. "Goddamn it, I'm so sorry." I hate that I'm still having these fucking nightmares. Doesn't matter how long I'm out of the fucking service, it's like I can't break free.

She doesn't say anything to me, but it doesn't look like she is angry either. In fact, I don't see any judgement in her eyes at all.

"Are you hurt?" I ask and force myself to stand up.

"No, I'm ok. Are you ok?" She asks.

"Yeah, what are you doing in here?" Why the hell was she even in the position where I would be able to get my hand around her neck?

"Like you said earlier you are right behind my wall. I heard you crying out and came in here to make sure that you were ok. I didn't expect you to wake up so upset. I've never seen anyone have a nightmare like that." She says before she turns around and takes a seat on my bed. Obviously just waiting for me to explain to her what was going on.

"Yeah, it's the leftovers from my time in the service. I always have the same dream ... Nightmare rather."

"Ah, I figured it was something like that. You kept saying get down. It was either that or you were talking to a kid." She shrugs and goes to stand up.

I grab her shoulder as she tries to walk by me. Instead of her fighting me off like I know she can do, she stops. Just looks at me, almost as if she is waiting for me to do whatever it is that I'm going to do to her. She trusts me. Why does that excite me so fucking much?

I trail my hand up her neck and over her chin before I take a step closer in her space. She doesn't move, doesn't even look like she is afraid. I trail my hand down the other side of her face before I lift her chin and check for myself that she is indeed ok. There are no bruises that I can see, but I just wanted to make sure.

"If this ever happens again, you don't fucking hesitate to protect yourself."

"I'm not going to-"

I cut her off before she can continue. I don't want to hear no shit about her not wanting to hurt me. I'm so much fucking bigger than she is, in the state that I was just in I could do some serious harm to her without ever knowing that I'm hurting her. That is the last thing I want right now. I know that she has the skill and strength to protect herself and I want to make sure that she does just that. "You protect yourself, understand?"

Her mouth snaps shut and she just glares at me for a second. "Yeah, I get it."

I nod my head and my eyes drift down to her lips. Fuck I want to feel them against mine. I know that my intense need for her is only because of the nightmare that I've just had. This happens all the time. My psyche fucking tortures me. I find a woman I can lose myself with and then I'm left unfulfilled and annoyed. It never becomes anything. I only want her, because she is standing in front of me. Though I have to say that I don't remember the last time I was as turned on as I am now.

"What are you looking at?" She asks and my eyes stay glued to her lips.

"You." I answer right away, there is no reason to lie.

"Yeah? And what exactly do you see when you look at me?"

"Trouble, nothing but fucking trouble." I back away from her and let my hands drop down to my sides. "You ready to go back to sleep?" I ask her suddenly wanting nothing more than to get her out of my space.

"Yeah, now that you are through screaming your ass off, I think that I can get some sleep."

"Harty har har, go to bed." I walk over to the bedroom door and open it for her.

She raises an eyebrow and walks out the door without looking back to me. I don't know if it's the tightness of my compression pants or the way she sways her hips from side to side, but I find myself staring at her ass as she makes her way back to her room. I need to stay the fuck away from her. I know I do, but I don't want to.

I'm too keyed up. There is no way that I'm going to be able to get back to sleep right now. I lay in the bed and think about this mysterious woman who literally dropped into my life. Celine is going to destroy me. I don't know how or why, but I know something about her is going to change me.

CHAPTER

11

JAMESON

"What the fuck did you roll up on last night?" Pirate asks as I walk into church. Everyone that is supposed to be here is already seated at the table just waiting for me to get Celine taken care of.

Our church is in the back of the compound. There is nothing behind the building, but trees and swamp. But that serves as a great buffer for anyone who might try to sneak up on us. Trekking through the fucking swamp is harder than you might think. It may be a nightmare outside, but inside the large room is absolutely mind blowing. Archer spared no fucking expense when it came to making sure our facility was top of the line. The entire building is fire retardant. The church itself has steel plate lined walls with another insulated wall of wood on top of it. Not only was it warm and soundproof, but someone trying to break down any of the walls would have a really hard fucking time. All of the windows are wired with motion detectors. There is also a complete wall that is nothing but mounted computer flat screens, with modems and hard drives all wired throughout. We use everything at our disposal to make sure we have all the information we need before we went out on a job or worked on a new business venture.

The prized piece though was the huge rectangular wood table in the middle of the room. The table itself was a complete replica of the original from the main chapter—an homage to home.

Archer, as the president, sat at the head of the table. My seat is on the left of Archer as the VP and Yang sits on the right of him as the Sergeant at Arms. Bones is on the right side as the Enforcer of the club.

Pirate sits next to me as the Treasurer. The rest of the patched in members are allowed in the church, but they stand. Archer is all about keeping things transparent in club business. The only ones that aren't allowed to know what is going on are the prospects, because they don't need to fucking know.

"That took you long enough, I thought maybe you were gossiping or some shit." Pirate jokes.

"Fuck that, she doesn't want to be bothered. I don't need her trying to skip out in the middle of the night, because she is scared of us or her surroundings."

"She spent the night with a bunch of dirty bikers, I think she already has enough to be worried about. Tell her to gut up." Bones shrugs his shoulders as if he doesn't care. I'm sure he doesn't. Bones doesn't care about much of anything.

"Whatever … Archer, what's up?" I'm ready to get to business.

"We need to come up with a plan to get this René bastard out of town."

"That shit isn't happening easily and you know it. We all know how much he controls around here." Pirate speaks up. As the treasurer he knew the ins and outs of the gambling scene. "René is high up on the totem pole. We're not going to be able to go in there and just force him to shut down, no matter what the fuck he is doing. I mean you all heard the girl, he is always surrounded by his cronies."

"Yeah, there has to be a way. I'm not just going to sit back and let him take whatever the fuck he wishes just because he controls some fucking fight club. That's not how this shit works." Archer spits out.

"I thought we weren't getting involved with business that wasn't our own. Isn't that what Clean ordered?" I hate how those words feel rolling off my tongue. Clean is the new president of the original WOD chapter. A seat I'm not a hundred percent convinced he is ready for, still he is our president. The only one over Archer himself.

"You think this isn't our business? How long before René sets his eyes on someone in our family? Daria? Capri? Tessa?" Archer leans forward and I can hear everyone shifting in their seats. Once you start talking about peoples' families, they tend to get much more invested. "Ignoring this isn't going to make the problem go away. We didn't go looking for this problem, we found it drowning in our fucking river. This is our problem now. Anyone have an issue with that?" Archer looks around the table and then around the room. No one dares to go against him.

"So how are we going to go about doing this then. You want to just take him the hell out? Or what?" Pirate asks.

"No, we can be gentlemen about this shit until he shows us that he can't be. Let's go see if we can get him to back the fuck off the easy way." Archer frowns as he looks down at the table. He knows this shit isn't going to go the way that he wants it to go. He has to give it a try though.

I find it absolutely amusing that he would think that someone as ruthless as René would be the same type of person to just tuck tail and run away. That didn't seem like something that he would do.

"Go upstairs and see if Celine is willing to go on a little trip tonight."

I bite the inside of my lips just thinking about having to go back upstairs to that woman and ask her to come with us. All of us know who René is, but none of us have ever actually seen him. She is the only one that we know for sure has seen Rene. She could point him out to us. Unfortunately for her there is just so much that could go wrong. If someone were to see her than we would have a whole new problem on our hands.

"Would she have to get out of the car?" I ask, hesitating to get out of my seat.

"How is that your concern?" Archer asks, his eyes squint at me as he waits for me to answer.

"Look man, I know she doesn't mean anything to us, but she has obviously been through a lot of shit. She doesn't need to be thrust back into that shit if she isn't going to feel assured that we can protect her."

"Then fucking protect her." Archer says in a flat voice.

"Wait, hold on how ..." I can't even put together the words to complain about that. How the hell did I get saddled with that detail?

"Look you're right ok, she is vulnerable right now. We told her that we wouldn't let anyone get to her, but you have a better relationship with her. All the big shit we'll handle, but the day to day is on you,

Jam." Archer claps me on the back and raises the gavel to slam it down on the table indicating that the business portion of the meeting is closed. Great, now she is my responsibility.

I push back my chair and start back on my way to Celine. This shit is going to be fun.

She agrees to go. It didn't even take much to convince her either. She was game the second that I told her that we would all be there and that we would make sure that she was protected. When I explained to her that we were going to give René the chance to just cease and desist, she actually started to laugh. Not cute girly giggles, but full on head tossed back belly laughs. She said that she had no problem showing us who he was, but she didn't know where he was and she also didn't think talking would do anything. None of us do, but Archer likes to make sure that we do everything the right way. This is his process—everything in its freaking place.

"How the fuck do you even know about this shit?' I speak through the in-helmet mike talking to Pirate. He knew exactly where René would be tonight. Apparently, there is a big fight going down.

"Are you kidding me? Do you know how much cash is being pushed around at this shindig? I always know where all the fucking money is." Pirate sniffs like he can smell the money in the air even though we are all riding slowly through the back streets of Bataria Drive.

"Hey, cut the fucking chatter and keep your damn eyes open." Archer barks into the mic and we all shut the hell up. There was no one in the world that could say Archer couldn't lead a fucking outfit.

Archer, myself, Shyne, Pirate, Bones, and Gator are all on our bikes while our two prospects Clay and Mark are in the car with Celine behind us.

"Holy shit." Shyne says as we pull up in the large parking lot. There was no reason for us to ride quiet. There are so many damn people here, no one would have even noticed us. How the police didn't come check this shit out was beyond me. It's like they didn't even want to admit that something like this was happening when they had the fucking lights blaring in their backyard.

"Archer, if shit goes bad we don't have much of an out." Bones speaks up as we roll to a stop. I look over to the car trying to catch Celine's gaze. She is looking in both directions.

"Copy." Archer says over the line.

We are going to need to get a lot fucking closer, but this is about as close as I want Celine to get. I don't want any of them to see her.

"Jameson, see if Celine can point him out from where she is." Archer speaks as he keeps his bike idling.

"Yeah."

The entire parking lot is covered with bright lights so the people in the center are completely visible. There are a lot of parked cars so there is some cover. Except I'm not sure that I can get Celine in a position where she would be able to tell us if one of the men there is René. I had an idea of who he was, but we needed to be certain.

I hop off my bike and rush over to her door. When I open it she quickly tries to get out, she knew what she was here for.

"Hold up." I put a hand out to keep her in the car.

"What's wrong?"

"I'm not going to let you go all the way down there. If I put you behind one of the cars do you think you would be able to see from back here. I'd prefer for you to stay as far away as possible."

She bites her lip for a second, "Who is going to watch your back?"

Huh. I didn't expect her to be worried about who is watching my back, but I guess it does make sense. I mean, I'm the only thing that she has that is close to an ally if I'm hurt, she is on her own again.

"Don't you worry about me darlin', I'm going to be fine." I grab her hand and we stay in cover, but I get her closer to another car that has a clear line of sight to the main area where the fights are taking place.

"That one, with the gray suit." She says immediately.

"Ok, that's what I thought, come on let's get back in the car." I rush and put her back in the car.

"Mark, Clay stay here with her." I order the prospects.

"Wait, don't you think you should stay back. Even just halfway?"

Celine looks around again, her fists balled up and the tension rolling up her clenched muscles.

"I can't I have to go in, but you can talk to me through the car communication system, we all have receivers in our ears. So if something is going on just let us know." I hope this is enough for her, because this is all that I can do right now.

She nods once and I make my way over to Archer. She doesn't get out of the car, but she stares at me as I move closer to danger.

"The one in the gray." I let Archer know as I come up behind him.

"Ok, everyone let's go."

We all leave our bikes parked and walk towards the densely populated area.

"What the fuck is this?" Shyne asks.

When I look around, I see a group screaming. There is a group of dudes in a royal rumble like brawl, everyone swinging and kicking each other. This is not just a hit until you are out of the space, they are beating people to death.

"Archer, he's not going to want to fucking talk. This man is out of his fucking mind." I whisper and try to move back.

"Jame-th-st-beh-"

There is some static coming in over the earpiece, but I can't make it out.

"Celine?" I whisper, but I don't hear anything back. "Clay?" When I don't hear anything come through I look over to where Archer is. "Something is up." He is pressing the receiver against his ear as well. He can't make out what is going on any more than I can.

"Get back over there." Archer stands up higher than he should and all of us see the one mark that says we are fucked—a bright red dot.

"No!" Shyne yells out and dives at Archer. The second they fall into the car, the window directly behind them explodes. A bullet slicing through the air only inches away from where Archer was standing. These bastards were shooting at us.

"Fuck, get back!" Archer assesses himself quickly, but this time he makes sure he stays in cover.

We all rush backwards, but if they know that we were here hidden among all these cars then there is a good chance that they already know that Celine is here.

"Goddamn it, Celine, fucking answer me." I try to pick up the pace, but before I can take another step a bullet ricochets off the back of the car I'm leaning against.

"Fuck it, open fire." Archer gets behind cover and starts searching for any of the shooters.

"It's a goddamn ambush!" Bones calls out and fires a few times.

These bastards were surrounding us.

"Jameson!" a garbled sounding Celine comes through my earpiece, but I can't move. If anything fucking happens to her I don't think I'll be able to forgive myself. I did this. I want to run to where she is, but all I can do is try to fight my way out of this.

CHAPTER

CELINE

I try to keep my eyes glued to Jameson's back, but they are soon weaving in and out of the parked cars and I can't follow.

"Relax, they know what they are doing." the one I think they call Clay says.

"Relax? Are you fucking kidding me? Do you think just because they are having an event in a parking lot these bastards don't know what they are doing? René isn't someone you want to underestimate." I roll my eyes and try again to find where Jameson is. I don't want to think that his leader doesn't know what he is doing. Despite that I have a feeling that he doesn't know how serious René is about his business. When Jameson told me that Archer wanted to talk to René, I wanted to tell him that there is no way that René will listen. René has visions of ruling all of the underground one fight at a time. There is no way that he is going to back off just because someone asks him to. No matter what show of force they have.

"Where are they?" I hiss out more to myself than anyone else.

"Ten o'clock." The one they call Mark says.

"What?"

"To the upper left." He points and my eyes follow his finger.

I'm surprised to find that I'm relieved. Jameson might be a little rough around the edges, but I know that he is being real with me. He wants to help me. In a world full of people that are only looking out for themselves, I found Jameson in the one moment of time that I needed him the most. "Ok, good. Now what are they doing?" I ask the boys in the front seat. Jameson and the rest of them all seem to be huddled down. It was like they didn't want to move forward. The fight was still going on too. René was still standing there. I can't see much of him, but I can pinpoint him.

"They must see something they don't like. Archer isn't going to walk into something that he doesn't feel we are prepared for. Archer is smart." Mark speaks highly.

My eyes move further to the left, away from the fighting that is happening in the brightly lit parking lot. Something is moving, a lot of something.

"Mark, do you see that? Something is moving over there. Can they see it?" I know getting excited is not going to do anything, but I have to warn them.

"Shit, that's not in their line of vision. They are all too bunched up. Fuck." Clay presses a button that activates the communication system that they all have hooked up.

"Archer? Archer, can you hear me?" There is nothing. No one answers.

"Oh no." I turn my head to the far right and I see more people moving in. They are caught, someone must have fucking saw them come in.

"Mark, we have to go in. Can you reach them?" Clay says and pulls out a weapon.

"What the fuck are y'all waiting on? Get the fuck out and help them!" This wasn't happening fast enough. They were all just sitting there talking about what should happen. When they should be out of the car and rushing over to help Jameson. Help their brothers.

I open the car door, but before I can take a step out someone reaches in and pushes me back into the seat by the throat. "Shit! Let me go!" I try to scream, but everything seems like it's muffled.

"Fuck off her!" Clay turns to help, but there is someone else at his window pulling him out and another on Mark's side.

"Would you look at this? René is going to be so happy that Thomas will get his gift after all. We knew you'd fucking come back, bitch." The man snarls as he presses himself down onto me in the back seat. It was the same man on the fucking ferry from last night. The one that had told me about what Thomas likes to do to the women that his father gives him.

I slam my head forward and I connect with his face. He pulls up and grabs at his face. "Fuck! I should kill you for that shit!" He barks, but he is off me far enough that I can crawl out from under him. I do just that and slither my way out the opposite door. As my body drops to the ground outside of the car, I hear a shot and the man that was holding Mark falls down in a heap.

"Shit! Hold on Clay!" Mark jumps over the hood of the car, all very action movie-esque, the gun he used to kill the man still in his hands. I scramble into the car and press down on the button that lets us talk to the rest of the guys. I scream for Jameson, but I don't hear anything in return. Clay and Mark fight back the two men that are here at the car. I grab a gun that one of the guards had dropped on the floor and run in the direction that I last saw Jameson and the rest of the boys. They are pinned in as a small half circle closes in on them. They won't last long in the position that they are in. I may not be the best shot, but I can aim and know which end of the gun is the dangerous one.

I aim at the back of one of the guards and pull the trigger. The bullet hits the mark though it's not a lethal shot. It's enough to get some of the guns that were trained on the boys to turn towards me. It's an opening. I find one other guard that I can shoot. This bullet doesn't hit, just bounces off the car right next to him. He turns to me as well.

"Back to the fucking bikes! Now!" I hear Archer yell out. More bullets fly, but now I realize that they are all aimed at me. I fall down and cover my head the best that I can. I scream and wait for the bullets to stop, but they never seem to.

I turn to see Mark and Clay, they are shooting and trying to get the few guards that are left away from the rest of guys.

It's working. I hear footsteps coming towards me and when I peek around the corner, I see all of the Wings of Diablo boys making their way over to their bikes.

"Come on!" Jameson stops right next to me and settles me on the back of his bike before he high tails it out of the area.

Mark and Clay jump back in the car and follow behind us. By the time we make it back to the clubhouse I can't fucking stop shaking. I barely wait for Jameson to pull to a complete stop before I jump off the bike and rush to the room that they let me have. I didn't run away from one dangerous situation to walk back into another one. My father had taught me better than this shit. What the fuck was I doing here?

"Celine, hold up." Jameson is rushing behind me. My leg hurts, but I don't slow up. I feel like a fucking idiot.

"No."

"What the hell do you mean no?" He grabs me before I make it into the room

"What the fuck do you think I mean? I said that I was planning to go back to my father this morning, but instead I let you talk me into going along with this stupid ass plan. I told you he wouldn't fucking listen. I told you that he wasn't that type of man, but your people fucking insisted. I just spent the last hour worrying about getting my damn head shot off. I don't need that kind of fucking stress. So no, I'm not going to slow up. I'm going to get whatever I have here and I'm going to go somewhere that I feel safe, with people who are going to be worried about my safety." I turn and try to open the door to the room. My knee buckles slightly and I hiss out in pain.

"What's wrong?" Jameson asks, but I don't answer.

I take another step and the same thing happens. I must have tweaked my knee. Now that I'm coming down from my adrenaline rush, I'm feeling all the pain.

"What's wrong?" He asks again, but this time his voice is louder than before. He isn't screaming at me, but I can tell that he doesn't want to be ignored.

"Nothing, I just hurt my knee a little, I think. I'm fine." I bend over slightly and try to massage the pain out of my leg. I hear a grumble. Although before I can even stand back up to ask him what he had said he already had me in his arms and is carrying me into the room.

"She good?" Archer asks from where he is standing in the main area of the club. Everyone is shaken up. I feel a bit like an asshole now that I realize that I'm making this all about me. They all were in the same fucking position. They could have all been killed right along with me. Fighting my damn fight.

"Yeah, I got her." Jameson replies before he carries me in the room and kicks the door closed behind us. He places me on the bed and hovers near me. "Let me see."

"What?" I ask and tilt my head to the side. What is he asking to see? There is nothing for him to see.

"The knee, show it to me."

"I can't get these tights up my leg." I explain.

"Take them off then. I want to see your leg." He doesn't give me the option to tell him no. I could fight him, but I know that no matter what I say he isn't going to back down. I'm used to testing everyone around me. I'm usually the one in control and command no matter what is going on, but Jameson's predominance has me falling into a role of submission. It's actually quite fucking annoying, yet intriguing. "Fine."

I stand up, but as I do my knee buckles again and I end up falling forward. Jameson is there to catch me before I can fall on my face. My leg must be more messed up than I think it is. I let my hands grip onto his arms, and against my better judgement I squeeze his biceps slightly. The man is huge with dark hair, dark eyes, scruffy beard and muscles everywhere. I don't think there is one soft place on his body. His eyes are intense, they tell a whole story that I'm just longing to hear. His hands grip me securely and his calloused skin scrapes against my smooth flesh.

"You got it?" He asks, the loud voice he spoke in before now softer.

"Yeah, I got it. Thank you." I pull out of his embrace and quickly slip my fingers into the waistband of the tights that he gave me to pull them down. I don't have any underwear, but this isn't the first time that he has seen me naked.

He pushes me down on the bed and grabs the sheet to drape over my exposed pussy.

He picks my leg up and those rough fingers that I had just tried to memorize on my arm slide there way over my legs. He presses down slightly on my knee and I flinch from the pain.

"I don't think it's broken or anything like that. Maybe just a bad bruise." He says before he let my leg go.

"What are we playing doctor now? Do I get to examine you this time?" I chuckle thinking back on the game I used to play when I was a child.

"You are free to examine me whenever you please, Darlin'." He shoots me a half smirk and I have to stop myself from lunging at him. Fuck this man was probably the most sexually charged person I have ever been in contact with in my life. I had to keep my eyes on the prize though. I had to make sure that I wasn't getting distracted by this hot man with all the charm. I stand up to get some distance between us, making sure to pull my pants on in the process.

"Sorry, that's not happening." I cross my arms over my chest and try to take a step back. "Are you going back to your room now or what?"

A knock on the door breaks the tension in the room. When I turn my head to see who it is, there is a slight woman standing there. Her eyes are wide and there is a splattering of freckles along her high cheekbones.

I don't know who she is. The fact that I'd yet to see another woman in this place made me uneasy from the get go.

"Daria, what you doing up so late babe?" Jameson walks over and kisses her on the cheek. Maybe this is his woman. I can't help the jealousy that surges to life in my veins. Why the hell am I jealous in the first place?

"Oh, you know I can't sleep when you boys are out. I had to make sure that he came home alright. You mind if I chitchat with her a bit? I have some stuff for her too." She shows her hands full with clothing and some food. Things I desperately need right now. Especially that food.

"Yeah, I'll go check in with Archer. Let me know if you girls need anything." Jameson shoots me a glance and then leaves the room just as quickly as we walked in.

"Sorry about this, I swear nothing was going on." She must be wanting to kick my ass. I know that if some girl was sitting down naked in front of my man, I would be more than just a little upset.

"Huh?" She asks.

"He was only looking at my knee, nothing else was going on."

She laughs slightly before she comes to sit down next to me. "Even if something were going on that is none of my business." She smirks at me and hands over the plate of food.

"Wait, what do you mean? I thought Jameson was your man?"

"No, not in the least. I'm married to Archer. Jameson is just my brother. I'm Daria by the way." She puts her hand out and I have to put the plate down to shake it.

"Oh, nice to meet you. I'm Celine."

"So how bad was it?" Her eyes squint and she bites the corner of her lip as if she is waiting for me to tell her bad news.

"It was the worst that I've ever experienced I'll tell you that." I look away for a second before I ask her, "If Jameson isn't your man then what is with the pet names? Babe?" I don't know why I care so much, it's none of my business.

"Oh, Jameson is just full of charm. Everyone is his babe." She smiles at me. "He is like that with everyone, though I have to say he is different with you."

Different? How? "What are you talking about? He isn't treating me any different?"

"Oh, you don't see it, but we all do. The hesitation, the protection, the trust, none of these are things that Jam gives away easy. He may seem like a real cold fish, but he is really warming up to you. I would even gamble that the man has a little bit of a crush on you."

Now it's my turn to chuckle, "Absolutely not. I'm a burden to him. Sure, he is doing what he has to do to keep me safe. But I'm sure he would rather be somewhere else doing anything else right now."

She stands up from the bed and leaves the pile of clothes there for me. "I can't disagree with you there. I just think that maybe he would like to be doing anything else right now as long as you are with him."

I open my mouth to retort, but she puts her hand up to stop me. "I get that you don't see it, but just be careful with him ok. The last woman he trusted tore him to shreds. Don't do that to him, ok. If the feelings aren't mutual just let him know and keep it simple."

I didn't know where she was getting her information from. There is no way that he has any type of feelings for me besides maybe anger and annoyance. I don't want to argue with her though. She was trying to help me so the least I can do is be nice to her in return.

"Ok, I'll do my best." I smile at her and she returns it before walking out. I could tell her a little white lie if it would put her mind at ease.

CHAPTER 13

CELINE

I spend the rest of the night too amped up to sleep. My knee hurt, but I force myself to walk back and forth in the small room to fight through the pain.

Walk it off, Celine.

That was my father's catch phrase when I was a child and got hurt. He wasn't much of a coddler and since my mother wasn't around, he'd taught me how to be tough. There wasn't one injury that I hadn't tried to walk off. After three or four dozen rounds of pacing the pain has diminished some.

"What are you doing?"

I jump when I realize that the door is open and Jameson is staring at me.

"The fuck!" My hand instinctively slaps to my chest as if I'm going to stop my heart from popping out of my chest. "Didn't you learn your lesson from last time! Knock!" I drop my hand down to my side and snarl at him. Luckily this time I'm not naked, but instead I am wearing the pajama set that Daria had left for me. It's much more comfortable than what Jameson had given me to wear.

"Well I knew you were awake, because it sounded like you were trying to wake the dead with your nonstop pacing. Do you ever sit still or is that just something you haven't learned?"

Damn, I didn't even think that anyone would hear me, but I guess I have been going at it for a little while now.

"Sorry. I can't sleep. I'm feeling a little anxious." I admit even though just saying the words are enough to get me to look down to the floor. I didn't like to feel weak or vulnerable.

"Would you feel better if I slept in here with you?" He asks his face completely void of any humor. Of course, I would think he was just trying to get in the same room as me so he could get in my pants. Except I can see from his face that he just wants me to be at ease, having sex with me is the last thing on his mind right now. I appreciate it, because he is right. I would feel much more secure if I were with someone that I trusted.

"Yes." I say on a breath.

He nods once and goes back in his room. He comes back a few seconds later with a blanket and a pillow. Laying them down on the floor, he turns his back to me. I can see the large dark blue splotches on his back. They must be bruises from the fight earlier this evening.

"You can sleep in the bed with me." My eyes open wide, I've never slept in a bed with any man besides my father before in my life. I know I'm only telling him that he can sleep in the bed with me, because I don't want him to get hurt any more. Still the ease in which those words came out of my mouth is astounding.

"I'll be ok on the floor." He continues to lay out his blanket. He isn't going to just give in. It feels like everything that happens between the two of us is a fight for power. This is one fight though that I'm positive that I'm not going to lose. I'm not going to give him the chance.

"Damn men, never fucking listen." I murmur under my breath and storm over to where he'd laid his stuff down. I pick up his pillow and toss it on the bed, opposite of my side. The bed isn't very big, a queen size only. It's big enough for the both of us to sleep comfortably though.

"Get in the bed Jameson. There is no need for you to sleep on the floor."

He sighs and makes his way over to the bed, "Whatever … just stop fucking pacing before you mess up your knee more than it already is." He murmurs before dropping himself down on the bed and pats the mattress so that I can join him. I give up and do what he asks. I lay on my back feeling stiff. I'm so uncomfortable that I don't fall asleep.

Instead, I just listen to his slow breathing as he falls asleep and envy him.

I take this chance to turn over and look at him. He is truly a beautiful man. His dark features are all completely relaxed as he sleeps semi-peacefully. I wish I could just get inside his head and figure out why he's trying so hard. I mean sure he could have cut me loose already. Having reached the limit of where most good Samaritans would have gone, but instead he has taken my fight on as his own. Why? Hhe doesn't know me from fucking Eve. He doesn't know my father either. All he knows is that I need help and he is willing to do it for me. He is the same way with the rest of the people in his club, willing to do whatever needs to be done to help them. It's so rare that you find someone of this caliber now a days.

"No, get down … fuck." He groans out and I can see the start of a nightmare begin. I know what is going to happen if I let him go all the way down this path. I don't want to startle him awake, but I also don't want his fucking hand around my neck again. I rub a hand down his arm and try to shake him awake, but it doesn't do anything. I put a bit more force into my movements, but he still doesn't wake. I move my hand up to the nape of his neck and pull slightly on the small amount of hair back there with one hand while I use the other hand to shake him again. Maybe if I put together a bit of pain with a shake, it'll get him to wake up.

"Jameson, wake up, you're having a nightmare."

Jameson gasps out and his eyes pop open. His hand wraps back around my neck, but this time on the back side. He pulls me down and kisses me softly on the mouth. A small squeak leaves my throat, but I don't pull away. I've always pulled away when someone has kissed me. I've had plenty of boyfriends in the past. Usually none of them make it past a week or two before we break up and one of the main reasons is because there's never any spark. One soft kiss from Jameson is enough to have electricity slingshotting through my whole body, different than anything I have ever felt before.

I don't know how to respond any more than just let him kiss me. Part of me is afraid that if I try to move or something like that the spell will be broken.

He kisses me again. A groan leaves his mouth and I can't help my own moan in return.

I feel his eyelashes fluttering against my skin and he jerks his head back, "Oh shit, Celine. I'm sorry. I was asleep. I didn't mean it."

He didn't mean it, that was probably the best kiss I have ever had in my life and he is telling me that he didn't mean to kiss me. I'm going to call bullshit on that. I don't know what is going on with us or if anything is going on at his end at all. Yet, there is no way that I am the only one who felt that spark.

I lean my face back down and press my mouth to his kissing him just as softly as he was kissing me a second ago. Goosebumps erupt on my arms as the same electricity that I'd felt moments earlier begins to zip through me.

If he didn't feel anything then he could pull away. He doesn't.

His hand grabs the back of my neck and he pulls me closer to him, the soft kisses turning into aggressive needy kisses. I push him down trying to get him in the position that I want, but he quickly twists and pulls me under him. He grabs one leg and pulls it up over his hip, the soft fabric doing nothing to buffer the feel of his hard dick in his own sleep pants. I'm so surprised when my hips start moving on their own. God, I want more of him. This is happening so fucking fast. I want to take control, it's just my way. My hands spread out on his skin, the muscles in his shoulders and back roll with every one of his movements. I scratch my hands down lightly, just to see if I can get him to moan like he did before. He hisses out a breath in pain and stops kissing me for a second and a deep growl vibrates in his chest.

"You know what you're doing darlin'?" His voice is gruff and strikes a chord deep inside me. Starts a burn that I know he is going to be able to snuff out.

"Not a clue? Am I doing something?" My hips buck up towards him again and his eyes close in something that looks close to agony. Despite that the sounds that leave his mouth make me believe that he likes it.

"Don't fucking play with me." His eyes open and they pin me down to the mattress. I'm playing a game I've never played before and as much fun as it is, I know that I'm not ready.

"Fine, you don't want to play than we won't play." I shrug and look away as if I'm no longer interested in what we were just doing even if my body is screaming for him to continue. I didn't get to twenty-three still a virgin if I wasn't able to deal with temptations. I would just have to handle things myself in the shower.

"That's a good choice. We need to keep our heads on straight until we figure out what is going on." It sounds like he is saying this more to himself than to me, so I don't respond. I'm sure anything that comes out of my mouth right now would be more of a temper tantrum than something that would be considered smart. I roll over to my side a bit unsure of what is supposed to happen next. He wraps his arm around my waist and pulls me against him. His body molding to my own and his way of telling me that he isn't angry that I've chosen not to keep going.

"Trouble." He mutters before I hear his breath even out and he falls back into sleep. I smile at the thought that I'm the one that is getting under his skin. This might not be the game that I'm used to playing, but I think I'm going to enjoy it.

CHAPTER 14

CELINE

The next morning when I wake up Jameson is no longer in the bed with me. It's an annoying feeling to wake up expecting something and it's not there. I hop into the shower and do the best I can to relieve some of my pent-up tension from last night. It doesn't take long and the images of Jameson that I have stored in my memory make it all the more pleasurable. The ache lessens, but it's not completely gone. I walk down the stairs to see Daria and another woman in the kitchen. They have the radio on, but its low. The two of them are cooking and the aroma of whatever they're making causes my stomach to growl in anticipation.

Daria sees me in the doorway and smiles. I return the gesture and make my way into the kitchen. These people have clothed me, fed me, fought for me, and even almost died for me. The least I can do is help make breakfast.

"Hey I'm Tink, I'm Shyne's cousin." She put her elbow out for me to bump since her hands were wrist deep in biscuit dough. I bump her elbow and introduce myself.

"Do you guys do this every day? I don't know what you are making, but it smells divine."

"Oh yeah, pretty much. I don't mind though; the men need to eat and if we leave them to their own devices, they would eat Chinese food day and night. I'd rather Luke not have a heart attack just yet." Daria giggles as she flips over some flapjacks before turning her attention to the link sausages in the pan next to it.

"Can I help?" I ask wanting to feel useful.

"Can you cook?" Tink asks her eyebrow raised in skepticism. For such a small woman I'm sure she was a handful.

"I'm no Emeril Lagasse, but I can hold my own."

"Girl, don't no one compare to Emeril! Make whatever you like." Tink said enthusiastically.

I go to the fridge and pull out what I would need for a good egg scramble. I get to work chopping up the veggies and swaying my hips to the music that they are playing. "Are the boys sleeping?"

"Oh nah, most of the guys here are ex-military so they are usually up with the break of freaking dawn. I never need an alarm clock with Luke." Daria laughs.

"Who is Luke?" This was the second time she had said that name and I didn't know who the hell it was.

"Oh sorry, you probably know him as Archer. Luke is his real name." She leans over and whispers, "Don't tell him I told you though."

We both start laughing like high schoolers. I take a chance and reach my hand over to where the radio is and turn it up a bit.

"Fuck that! If you going to do it, do it all the way!" Tink reaches back over and turns the radio all the way up. The loud music distorts slightly as it makes its way through the tiny speakers.

"Wooo!" She takes her hands out of the dough. Her small frame starts spinning around, moving her hips in small circles doing her best to imitate the one and only Shakira since her song is playing.

"What the hell is going on in here? I thought we was getting some food. I didn't know there was going to be a show as well." Pirate sticks his head through the small window that leads from the main area into the kitchen. There's a toothpick in his mouth and a smile on his lips as he watches Tink gyrate and swing around.

"You like that baby?" Tink shoots a wink to Pirate that has me wondering if she is with him. He seems to be in his early forties. Though I'm not one to judge someone based on age, as long as both parties are legal that is all I care about.

A loud gagging sound erupts from the side. I turn to see Shyne and Jameson standing at the door watching her.

"What the fuck are you doing? Having a seizure?" Shyne makes fun of his cousin.

"Don't hate, just because you don't have any rhythm doesn't mean that you can't appreciate that I do. I'm the best dancer in the family and you know it."

"Yeah, I also know that we have no dancers in our family. So, you might be the best of the absolute worst."

"That doesn't say much about you," I chime in even though it's clear that he wasn't talking to me. I've never been a shy person. Just because I was taken and forced to do shit that most people have nightmares about doesn't mean that it would change who I was. In fact, it's only spurred me to enjoy life more. "I mean, last I heard women like a man who knows how to keep a good rhythm." I shrug and look away.

"Oh!" Tink put a hand over her mouth and laughs loud. "You hear that shit Shyne, she said your stroke is wack!"

"What the fuck! That is not what I meant. I can hold that rhythm. I can hold it all night long!"

"Bro?" Pirate stares at him with a disbelieving smirk.

"Who you lying to?" Jameson says right next to him.

"Ok, fuck, I can keep the damn rhythm for a good hour. Then I'm gonna need a sandwich or something."

I throw my head back and start to laugh right along with everyone in the kitchen. A Dua Lipa song comes on the radio next. I love her and the music basically forces my body to move. I put the knife down and grab hold of Daria who is starting to dance. The both of us dance with Tink, having a good time, doing silly moves until Daria's attention is completely diverted. Somehow, Archer had strolled into the kitchen without any of us realizing and pulled up a chair. Daria's entire body turns to him as if he blew an imaginary whistle that only she can hear.

"Don't you two start this shit again. My boyfriend isn't here." Tink whines and continues to dance with me.

"What shit?" I ask moving my eyes from the scene playing out between Daria and Archer, and back to Tink.

"Huh, you'll see." She laughs before she grabs my hand and we do a silly spin.

Now Daria and Archer are in my direct line of sight and I can already tell what she is talking about. The sexual tension in the room rose from nonexistent to suffocating. Daria keeps eye contact with her husband and she moves her body sensually as he stares at her. I wait for his expression to crack, wait for him to lose control like I've seen so many men do in the past. He doesn't.

Daria does a sexy move where she has to bend forward and put her arms on his shoulders. Her small breasts now fully on display for him and him alone. It tips the scale. Archer pulls her hard. Hard enough that she falls on his lap. He slaps her hard on her ass and her head falls into the crook of his neck. He uses his free hand to hold her tight to him as he whispers something in her ear. I watch her hand tighten and a blush crawl up her neck. I can only fucking imagine what the hell he is saying to her.

"See I told you." Tink says from next to me.

I laugh slightly, but it's a bit more breathy than my usual. I want to know what he is saying to her.

"Seems like you need something to distract you a little bit."

My head turns to the side and I catch Jameson just as he slips his arm around my waist and pulls me closer to him. It's amazing how quiet he is for such a large man. As he starts to move to the beat of the song it's also surprising how graceful he is. It takes but a second for me to completely forget about what was going on with Archer and Daria, as he leads me in a sensual dance. More of a rocking of hips, but with every dip and swivel my body moves right along with his.

"Looks like you can keep a good rhythm." I whisper, and have to stop myself from slapping a hand over my mouth. My cheeks burn with embarrassment, but he doesn't laugh.

He leans his head lower so that his mouth is near my ear, "I'm beginning to think you want to find out firsthand."

A small gasp leaves my mouth, but I'm quick on the draw, "And if I do?" I lean my head back and gaze into his eyes. I want to see how far I can push him. Testing limits is in my DNA.

"Darlin, that is something I can deliver." He pulls me closer to him so I can feel his dick pressing into my abdomen. I don't know the average size of a man, but it surely doesn't feel like he is below average.

"See I told you." Daria says from behind me and it's her voice that breaks the spell that Jameson has me under.

When I turn to look at her, I can see the cheeky grin on her face.

"You told me what?" I turn in Jameson's grasp

"You know exactly what I told you. Keep denying it if you want to." Daria shrugs and turns back to Archer.

Of course, I remember what she'd told me. She told me that Jameson was opening up to me, that he was closer to me than he let on. I'd told her it was bullshit, but even I know from the way he is holding me that he is feeling something. It could be purely lust, but it could be something else.

"What kind of shit is this? Everyone all boo'd up and I'm here slaving over a hot stove alone." Tink rushes back to the flapjacks that Daria had left in the pan, from the color on them they were just a few seconds away from being overdone.

"Oh crap, I'm coming." I pull away from Jameson and feel a small twinge of disappointment that I can't stay in his arms longer. I'm going to need to figure out what is going on with him and I'm going to need to do it soon.

CHAPTER 15

JAMESON

We sit down in the main area to eat our breakfast, it's nothing new. Usually when there are no issues going on with club business, this is how we start every day. Family sharing laughs and food.

It's one of the reasons when Archer called me to join his club that it was a no brainer. Family means everything to me, and my brothers are my family. Most of the patched in members had been in the military even if it was just for a few months. Something about going through that experience really brings who a person is to the surface. Either the military turns you into a better man or it makes you worse. Sometimes it's a bit of both. Being in the military showed me that I would give anything to protect my family and that I would do anything to be a part of one.

When I look around the table watching everyone stuff their faces and talk enthusiastically. It's hard for me to believe that just last night we were in a fire fight with the guards of one of the most notorious names in the underground world here in New Orleans. Sure, it's something that we are going to have to deal with, but right now we were safe and enjoying our food.

I stab my fork into the remainder of the egg scramble that Celine had made and just like the first fucking bite my taste buds erupt in pleasure. God, that woman can cook.

My eyes dart up to her, but she is engrossed in a conversation with Tink. That's okay, gives me a good chance to just observe her. She has to be one of the strongest willed women I have ever met in my life, challenging doesn't even begin to describe her. Last night when I heard her screaming for me through the mic it felt like my soul was being ripped out of my body. I'd promised her that I was going to take care of her and I didn't. In fact, when we were all pinned down, I was almost positive that at least one of us was going to go down, but it was her that saved us. She'd distracted the guards enough so that we could make a run for it. She had saved me when it was supposed to be me that saved her.

I guess she could sense that I was staring at her, because her eyes dart up to mine. She startles when she sees that I'm looking at her. Her eyes squint in my direction when she realizes that I'm not going to look away.

She shakes her head like she is confused and flustered when she finally looks away from me. Whatever, Tink is no longer her focus. I'm getting to her. I don't stop staring at her and the increasing flush on her cheeks amuses me. For someone who is all grit and fight, she sure does get worked up quite easily. I watch her continue to try and keep up with the conversation she is having with Tink. Occasionally, she will touch her face or hide behind the honey brown shield that she calls hair. None of that shit stops me though. I like her squirming, it's quickly becoming one of the best parts of my day.

"Erm, I think I must have eaten too much. I'm just going to get a bottle of water." Celine gives Tink a soft grin, but doesn't bother to look at me.

"Oh, ok. Take your time." Tink turns and starts talking to Shyne.

My eyes follow Celine as she gets up from the table and walks toward the kitchen in the back. She's only been here a few days, but it feels like she belongs here. Her fists are balled up, and though I know she has been in the kitchen several times already she seems unsure of herself.

I push my plate away and stand up quickly.

"Where the fuck do you think you are going?" Bones asks me, a toothpick and a sly smile on his lips.

"I'm thirsty."

"Yeah, thirsty for some of that girl's pussy." He laughs and I kick him in the ankle as I move away from the table to follow Celine. She doesn't turn. I stop to examine her again when she gets around the corner to the entrance of the kitchen and she stops.

Her tension is off the wall and it seems physically strenuous for her to relax her shoulders. That shit makes all the fucking sense in the world, she was just in a fucking fire fight, an underground crime lord is searching for her, wanting to give her to his son, and she is separated from her family. I would be going crazy with tension as well. I take another step so I'm no more than one step behind her and I wait. She rolls her shoulders slowly then tilts her neck from side to side while she takes one last cleansing breath. She turns around and slams straight into my chest.

"You seem to be looking for something?"

"No, I just wanted something to drink. I wasn't snooping or anything like that." Her newly relaxed shoulders stiffen back up now that she thought she was in trouble.

"Ah, well the water is this way." I reach over her shoulder making sure to get as close to her as I can without actually touching her. Her lips quiver as she raises her head in my direction. "Unless of course you were waiting for something else."

"What would I be waiting for?"

"I think you were waiting for me, but I'm not sure." I take another step forward and even though she tries to stand her ground, she has no choice but to back up. I keep moving forward until she is flush against the wall and I have one hand over her head. "Darlin', I'm not the type of man that plays games. I know you've been through some shit, but I don't usually wait when I want something."

Her bottom lip shoots out and she softly wets it. I groan and move in closer. The fucked up shit about how crazy she is driving me is that she doesn't even seem to realize she is doing it.

"I have something you want?"

"Fuck yes." I grunt before dropping my mouth to hers quickly fusing our lips together. I bite and lick at her lips as my tongue glides across hers. Her breath is coming quickly as she threads her hands behind my neck and up into the scruff of my hair. She holds onto me tight and moans every time I pull away slightly. The shirt that Daria gave her to wear gets the job done in keeping her clothed, but its thin enough that I can feel how hard her nipples are.

"You're so damn sexy." I mutter and let my hands push their way under the shirt. Her skin is smooth and taut. Her body arches slightly as I drag my hand up towards her chest. If she wants me to stop she better say something, because until she does I'm going to keep going.

"Jameson. I don't ... I" She whimpers and this is the most vulnerable I have ever heard her. It fans the fucking craving that I have for her into overdrive.

"Shh, don't think. Just let me fucking take care of you." I grab hold of her face and tilt it to the side so that I can get to her neck. I suck hard on that smooth bit of flesh as my other free hand massages her nipple.

She grabs onto my shoulders and squeezes hard, trying to pull me even closer to her. If I get any closer, we'll be fucking. Not that it's something I'm against. I just don't think she is going to want to fuck when my brothers are just a few feet away from us.

When her hips start swaying, I pull away for a moment and grab her around her waist. Fuck this, my cock is too damn hard to be having a damn make out session. I want to feel her pussy wrapped around me. I lift her so that her legs are wrapped around my waist and I can take her to my room.

"Jameson!" Pirate calls out for me.

No! If there was any fucking day, I wished I was fucking deaf it was right now.

"What!" I scream back not putting her down. When she drops her face against the side of mine and starts to nibble softly on my ear, I almost drop her. "Dammit, Darlin' ... you're fucking killing me. Hold on." I squeeze her ass in my hands massaging the round tight globes that are waiting for me beneath her pants.

"Come on, we got company."

Fuck, this shit can't be happening right now. She giggles slightly which turns into a depressed cry. "I guess it's not meant to be." She kicks her feet a few times and I have to let her go. She slides down and her core puts pressure on my already painful dick. The last club bunny that I had did nothing to satisfy me. Just kissing Celine had turned me on more than I was turned on the entire time I was fucking that other woman.

"Fuck that, we're not through here. Let me just check whatever this shit is and then we going to finish what you started."

She rolled her eyes to the ceiling and a playful grin crosses her face, "Promises, promises."

I inch back towards her, but know if I start touching her again that I'm not going to stop.

Pirate wouldn't have called me if it wasn't something that I needed to be present for. Whoever is here better have something good to fucking say or I'm going to be pissed the fuck off.

CHAPTER 16

CELINE

I keep the smirk on my face as I watch him fix his pants and his shirt, so it doesn't look like we were back here making out like a bunch of teenagers. I don't want him to see how devastated I am that we aren't able to finish what we just started. I don't know what is happening with me. Except it feels like every one of the emotions that I never experienced in high school had surged to the surface the second he slid his hand under the fabric of my shirt. I want him. Fuck do I want him.

"Come on." He puts his hand out, not bothering to see if I wanted to go with him. He expected it. In fact, he commanded it. I want to stand there just because he is ordering me to do something. Despite that I cede, putting my hand in his and he tugs me behind him.

We didn't have sex, but just that small bit of excitement has me feeling like I'm in a sexual haze.

"Jameson, this man says he needs to speak with Celine." Shyne says and just like that the bliss I was feeling evaporates.

I look around Jameson's shoulder and can see one of René's guards.

"Oh no." I mutter and take a few steps back.

"Hey, what the fuck is going on?" Jameson turns to me and tries to grab my hand again. I rip it away. I have to run. I have to get the hell out of here. The man they'd let in was one of the guards that was supposed to watch me on the boat.

"You're giving me back?" My voice cracks with the terror I'm trying to keep at bay. Did they think that the fight last night was too much? Was protecting me not worth it?

87

"What? No. What are you talking about?" Jameson takes another step towards me.

"He said he's your friend, that he has a message from your father." Shyne speaks up, clearly confused about what was going on with me.

"The fuck he is! He is no friend of mine." I snarl out before I turn back to look at Jameson, "He's one of the guards that kept me locked up for René." I hiss at him.

"The fuck?" Pirate pulls out his weapon and aims it at the man.

Everyone in the room that is armed pulls out their weapon while the others move to protect the women.

"You must be out of your fucking mind coming in here. What the fuck did you think was going to happen, we would just let you walk out of here with her?" Archer spits out.

The guard stares at me. "You have to go back. There is no choice." the man speaks, but it's not as forceful as I would have thought and even a tear falls from his eye.

"I won't."

"You have to. René will kill everyone, people you don't know, people you do, until someone brings you back to him. He knows it was this club that was there last night and he knows that you are here. You have to go back."

"You can kick bricks you piece of shit. Tell your boss that Celine is with us now and she's not going anywhere." Jameson grabs the crook of my arm and pulls me backward.

"Get the fuck out of here before I make you regret waking up this morning." Bones snarls at the man.

"I already regret it." The guard whispers. "I can't leave without her." he says it louder so everyone can hear him.

"Fine, let's do this the hard fucking way." Yang takes a few steps forward, but before he can get close to the guard the man starts stripping off his clothes. "Yeah, I don't know what the hell-"

Yang didn't finish the words that were coming out of his mouth. Instead, he just gapes as the man stripped down to a t-shirt with a full abdominal cast of what looked like grey play doh. It was only when I saw the flashing lights and the small digital clock taped to his chest that I realize what the hell I'm looking at. That whole cast is a big fucking bomb.

"Oh shit! Oh fucking shit!" Everyone backs away from him quickly.

"I can't leave here without you and I can't stay." The guard says and more lights begin to flash. "If you don't walk out that door with me, they are going to detonate it. If anyone tries to leave, they will detonate it. You have to come with me."

I look around the space and see everyone that is there. I can't let them pay the price for my father's sins. Me, fine, but not them.

"Ok, I'm coming."

"The fuck you are!" Jameson barks and grabs me tighter. I try to pull away from him, but his grip is strong.

"You have to let me go, that shit will kill everyone in here. I have to go." I pull again, but he doesn't let me go.

"No!" he shouts at me.

I pull and kick, doing everything I have been taught not to do in a situation where I'm being held as the tears and fear take over any logical thought I had. "Let me go! Let me go right fucking now! You can't do this!"

Yang rushes over to where I am and tries to help Jameson hold me back. I hear more screaming as the lights on the man's chest begin to flash faster giving us all an ominous warning that it's about to blow up.

"Archer we have to get the fuck out of here!" Pirate yells out pulling the girls with him.

"No! It'll blow!" The guard cries out. His eyes scan the crowd quickly before it lands on Archer. His eyes bounce down to the tag on his kutte that says president and then back up. "Take me out ... please." The man says quickly.

"What?" My heart is bursting out of my chest. "No, just let me do this. No one has to fucking die! Let me go." I pull harder. This can't be fucking happening.

"Come on man, I don't want to go out like this. Just fucking kill me." the guard looks again at Archer.

"Shit!" Archer takes Shyne's weapon and aims it at the man's head. "How much longer?"

"Three minutes tops." The man says and closes his eyes. He is already resigned to the fact that he was about to die.

I'm still trying to break free. I don't want anyone to die even if he is a shit and I don't want to have anyone kill for me. I don't want any of this. "Please let me go!" I finally turn to Jameson and stare at him for a second. I want him to see the pain I feel at this moment. He doesn't budge.

"Sorry Darlin', that's not happening." He speaks softly, but shows no hint of easing up.

I let my head fall; I've never been so defeated in my life.

A lone shot rings out and suddenly there is a flurry of action. The minute the man falls down to the ground everyone runs over towards him pushing the rest of us away.

"Clay! Come now!" Archer bellows out. "Go get him right the fuck now."

Yang rushes into the back and he literally comes back out dragging Clay behind him. They'd woke him up to die.

"Oh shit! What the fuck?" When the young prospect looks over and notices the mound of flesh with the bomb on the floor, he rights himself to run over and drop down near the body. He works fast tugging and pulling out wires.

I look over my shoulder and stare at the young kid before I turn my attention back to Jameson. I'm sure every second that passes will be my last, thinking every time Clay moves the bomb it will go off.

"What is he doing? Why is he messing with it?"

"Clay is probably the only one here that can shut that shit off. He was an EOD specialist in the service, how he got his name. Claymore."

He's breathing fast, but he makes sure to send me a wink before he focuses back on Clay.

"Secure!" Clay calls out and raises his arms above his head as if he just finished a test.

"Get this bastard the fuck out of here. Clay get those explosives off. Yang, Shyne, Pirate, take your asses outside and see if anyone is around. Jameson get Celine together." Archer barks his orders quickly and everyone moves to do what he says. I throw my hands up and make my own way to the room that they are allowing me to stay in. They are trying to secure their clubhouse, but what fucking good is that going to do when the reason everyone is gunning for them is sleeping in one of their beds. As long as I'm here, none of them are safe.

CHAPTER 17

JAMESON

"Celine, hold up a second." I double check that everyone in the club-house is safe and then I turn to make my way to her. She is moving quickly towards the bedroom. I have a feeling that if she makes it there before I get to her that I won't be able to talk to her again this morning.

"Celine?" I call out again, but still she doesn't stop.

"For fuck's sake, just hold the hell up Celine!" I catch up to her just as she is walking into the room and trying to slam the door shut. I block it from closing with my forearm. She pushes hard, but even with all her weight she isn't stronger than me.

"Just go back outside." She barks at me and glares like she expects me to react to the aggression in her tone.

"I'm not fucking going anywhere. What the fuck are you playing at?" I snap right back at her.

"Jameson, you can't be that fucking dumb. I know you see what is going on here. Don't come in here and try to get me to ignore what just happened." She flings her hand in the air like she is dismissing me. That shit isn't going to fucking fly, I will not be dismissed. I know exactly what the fuck happened out there. I also know that she was willing to just give herself up even though we had her covered. I want to know fucking why.

"That is exactly why the fuck I'm asking you what the hell is going on, because I don't want to ignore what the fuck happened outside. Why in the fuck were you going to go with that bastard?"

"Why? Are you serious?" She squints her eyes at me before she takes another step in my direction and crosses her arms over chest. "Tell me Jameson before I showed up how many people have walked into your clubhouse with enough fucking explosives on their chest to blow up the entire building?"

"None." I answer right away since it wasn't something that has ever happened to us before.

"Precisely that shit never happened, and it probably would have never happened if your club didn't put your necks on the line for me. It's not just fucking you now either. It's all of them, Archer, Daria, Pirate. All of them out there that can potentially die, because of my family's fuck up. I can't live with that shit, Jameson. You told me earlier that you didn't play games, well this is one fucking game I don't want to play. When it comes to your safety and your family's safety, I won't fucking risk it." I watch her eyes flood with tears, but she refuses to blink and release them. Her jaw clenches tight and she just stares at me waiting for me to say something that would make her fight.

"Fuck woman, where the hell did you come from"?" I grab her neck and pull her towards me. She gasps in surprise before I slam my lips against hers. Her eyes slam shut and two big tears slide down each side of her face. She was willing to give herself up to make sure that we are okay. She is willing to lay her life down on the line for family. Our mouths move together like they were molded to be together, a perfect fit. Our tongues fight and entwine inside the warmth of our mouths while my hands roam freely on her ass and hips. Before our visitor I was already ramped up with my desire for her, but now isn't the time. She tries to latch on to my arms as I push her backwards.

"Celine, darlin' listen to me." I bend slightly so that I'm at eye level with her. I don't want her to miss a fucking word that comes out of my mouth. "You will never do some shit like that again. I gave you my word that I would protect you, my club gave their word. We knew what we could get into when we chose to do that. I can appreciate you wanting and willing to make sure that no one loses their life over you. But if you even attempt to walk out of this clubhouse and sacrifice yourself," I grab a handful of her hair and pull back so I can stand up straight and look down on her, "I will walk through fucking hell to bring you back. I'll kill anyone who gets in my way, more lives lost, more fucking nightmares. Don't force me to do that shit." I growl at her and her mouth gapes open slightly. I wait for her fight, knowing she wants to. I can see the fire in her eyes—the flames of defiance. Instead of the fight though, she closes her mouth and nods once.

"Thank you, Darlin'." I bend down once and kiss her tenderly this time.

"I hate this shit. I truly do." She exhales and closes her eyes. The weight of the day heavy on her shoulders.

"We all do, but we do what we have to do for those that we care about."

"Hmm, so you care about me?" she smiles and bites her bottom lip.

"I don't know what to call it, but I think Daria believes I do."

She chuckles, "Yeah. She told me to be careful with you."

"What the hell does that mean? Like I'm fragile or some shit?" What the fuck was wrong with me that Daria had to warn people to be nice to me.

"She seems to think that you are closed off to people and that I was getting under your skin."

"Closed off is one way to describe me with women, I guess I can see why she would say that."

"Why? What closed you off?" Celine walks to the bed and sits down, but keeps her undivided attention on me.

"Well, if you would have fucking been here for the shit show that was Monica than you would know why I'm closed off. I have a hard time trusting women. My ex cheated on me while I was deployed, I came home and caught them in our fucking bed together."

She hisses out in mock pain, "Ouch. That must have been rough."

"It was, but my dumbass wanted it to work. I thought I loved her, but I never trusted her again after that. We got divorced, but once she found out that I was part of this club she's upped her desire to get back with me. It's not just her either. Every woman I've been with always seem like they are after something else. Usually, I don't mind because I know for sure they won't be getting anything from me, but it's also caused me to be a bit stand offish with women." When I look at her again, she is looking at the floor kicking her foot.

"Sounds like you have a lot of women." She looks back up at me and gives me a sheepish smile.

Fuck, it did sound like I said I had a boatload of women waiting around. "Oh hell no, I'm not down with no shit like that. Having a woman is hard damn work, if I'm not sure I want to take on all that fucking responsibility I don't even let them think they have a chance with me. I'm free and clear."

"What about your ex-wife? You said she is still around. I don't think it would be wise for you to um ..." She looks around like she is a bit uncomfortable, "Maybe nothing should happen with us, if you are still going back and forth with her." Her eyes catch mine and latch on.

I sit down next to her on the bed and pull her so that she is turned slightly toward me, "Celine, Monica is nothing to me. I don't even let her come inside the clubhouse. When I'm with someone, I'm completely fucking exclusive with them. I don't like to share what belongs to me."

"Don't like to share? Me neither. It's all mine." Her lips barely part as she speaks those broken words to me and her eyes focus back on my lips.

"What's that there, Darlin'? You think you fucking ready for that responsibility?" I question her keeping my face as blank as possible. She nods her head, yes.

"I hope you fucking realize what you are saying. I tried to leave you the hell alone, because I promised you that I would keep you safe. Me fucking your brains out isn't supposed to be in that plan. Me ramming straight through you as your cunt tries to milk me dry isn't supposed to be what you are here for. I'm jealous as fuck, possessive and take when I want something to be all mine. So be fucking sure that you want that."

When she's whimpers and nods yes again, I know that I'm fucking lost. I hadn't wanted anyone like this since Monica. That shit had ended bad and just like every dumb ass cliché I promised that I would never even want to do that shit again. Only Celine has me going back on my word. I trust her already and I've never felt that she was after something other than staying safe. If that is the price I have to pay to get with Celine, I'd pay immediately.

CHAPTER

18

CELINE

"Jam, you in there?"

I turn my head to the side and start laughing, we had just started kissing again and it seems like fate just doesn't want us to get any further than second base.

"What the fuck! What?" Jameson slams his hand down on the bed next to my head.

"I'm sorry, Archer says you are supposed to come back out." Clay is the one talking through the door. Suddenly I need to get up. He is the one that was closest to the danger, the bomb. That last few minutes could have ended his life.

I push Jameson off me and pad my way to the door. When I swing it open Clay takes a step back, startled by the sudden movement. "Hey, you ok?"

"Hmm, yeah." Clay tries to smile, but the vein on the side of his neck is still pulsing a mile a minute.

"You sure? I mean that shit was intense. Jameson told me that you did that kind of stuff in the military?" I didn't want to pry if he didn't want me to pry, but I didn't want him to have to think about that trauma alone if he didn't want to either.

Jameson walks out the door bending low to kiss my neck once before he leaves the two of us in the doorway. "Hey, no men in my fucking room. You get it?" He says, slightly turned back in our direction.

I pull on Clay's arm and smirk, but Jameson isn't playing. I honestly feel like if I was in the room alone with Clay right now, he would lose his shit. It doesn't even matter if its someone he knows. If we are going to have a shot at whatever is going on between us than he is going to have to tone that shit down. I'm a grown ass woman if I want to be in the same fucking room as a man than I will. I'm a boxer for Christ's sake and most of the people I know are men.

I roll my eyes and let Clay go. The young prospect's eyes dart nervously between Jameson and me. When Jameson continues to walk away Clay takes a deep breath, but makes sure to take a step back from me.

"Don't worry about him, he's not going to do anything." I say, leaning against the door so he knows we aren't going inside.

"Ok, I don't want to make him mad. They already have it out for us prospects, because of all the little fuck ups, I don't know if Mark is going to make it."

"What? Why?"

"He let a man with a bomb strapped to his chest walk into the clubhouse. He was on watch, that is something he should have caught."

"Yeah, but the bomb was molded to his body. How was he supposed to know?"

"I hope they see it like that." I don't think I have ever seen someone so desperate to get into a club before and I went to a high school where there were three levels of cheerleader.

"You did a lot of work with bombs before?"

"Yeah, that's why they call me Clay. I was tasked with finding and dismantling any mines or bombs that were in my unit's way. It's a quick job one way or another. Either I get it done or I'm dead." He shrugs.

"That's fucked up. I'm sorry you had to do that for me. I'm sure you never want to see another bomb again."

"What?" He gazes at me for a second like he is trying to figure out how to say whatever he wants to say next, "If you are with Jameson, and it seems like you are, then you are one of us now. I'll look at a million bombs a day if it meant that I could be part of this family and keep them safe."

My eyebrows hitch up, the level of loyalty this group of people have is uncanny.

"Well thank you anyway, and don't listen to Jameson, if you want to come talk to me, I'm always here." I pat him softly on the shoulder. He nods his head once before he turns and walks back in the opposite direction. I lean against the door for a few more minutes just trying to think on what has happened in the last few days. My life had gone from calm and repetitive to complete chaos. I know Jameson will do his best to keep me safe, but there are so many elements that are out of his control. So many people that can be hurt—him, his club, their families, my father.

I still haven't been able to get in contact with my father. I believe in my heart that he is still alive, but doubts and panic are starting to creep in. What if they got to him before he could get out of town? What if they are hurting him to get me to come back to Thomas? René was willing to send one of his own in here to die, to try and draw me out so I know he could be doing that or worse to my father.

There is a footfall on the opposite end of the hallway and I see a body coming around the corner, "Celine, come on baby." Tink is standing by the corner and is beckoning me towards her.

"What's going on?" I hurry towards the pissed off looking woman.

"Archer is about to start giving his orders, looks like we are going into a lock down."

"Lockdown? What the hell is that?"

"I'll let Archer fill you in." Tink nods before she takes my hand and we make our way into the main area. All the members are there, the women and even a few people I didn't recognize.

"Celine, have you been able to contact your father?" Archer asks me before I have time to even get myself all the way settled.

"No, his phone keeps on ringing, but no answer yet. I should go by the house, maybe he lost his phone."

"Absolutely not." Archer says quickly dismissing my idea.

I open my mouth to retort, but a sharp tug on my hand gets me to shut up. Jameson is by my side and trying to signal that now is not the time to put up a fight. I don't think I will ever understand the politics that go along with being in a motorcycle club.

"We found evidence that tells us that there were at least four other people camped outside. The tracks aren't fresh either which means that René has people watching us. I know you all like your freedom, but I will not risk any of you being hurt or taken, because we are not being as safe as we should be. I'm calling a lockdown."

A rolling wave of groans and expletives come from the small crowd in the room.

"Hey! Shut the fuck up! Your president gave a damn order, suck it the fuck up and accept it." Bones yells out, cracking the verbal whip and getting everyone to stop their protests.

"I get it, trust me. I don't want to be stuck here or anywhere for that matter, but it's better to be safe than sorry. Get your families here and anyone you think could be a target, bring them here. We have more than enough room and if we don't, we will make some. Celine, I know your father is paramount to all of this, but once I call lockdown, you're not going to be able to leave. Keep trying him on the phone and any other way that you think you might be able to reach him. I don't want you to stress about him through all this." He nods once to me, but then continues to talk to the rest of the patched in members. "If something needs to happen outside, we will have back up at all times. If you go to the fucking corner store to get a beer you need to have at least four motherfuckers with you. Everyone understand?"

"Yeah."

"What about René? I don't think he is going to just back the fuck off this. What are we going to do about him?" Yang asks.

"We are just going to have to teach him some manners. Let's worry about getting all of our loved ones here first, then we can focus on a plan to take him the fuck out." Archer may not be the biggest man in the room or the loudest, but something about his persona demands obedience. His very aura is dominating.

"Yang get it together, I want the doors closed by 8 pm tonight."

With that everyone broke off into little packs to get the clubhouse ready for what was turning out to be a really long ass sleepover.

The club moved fast. From the minute Archer told everyone to get their people inside, the doors have not stopped opening. I stayed on the phone trying to reach my father. Jameson was still against me going over there in person to see if he was at home. He said that its the first place René would send someone to look for me.

He did promise me that he was going to swing by there, just so he could check the place out. If he saw my father, he would bring him back with him.

"Celine, you got everything you need? Anything I can send the prospects to the store for?" Daria asks as she trudged up towards me with a bag of groceries in her arms.

"No, that's ok. I don't have any money."

She rolls her eyes, but smiles sweetly at me. "I don't need any money from you. Just tell me what you need and we will get it for you."

"Well, I could for sure use some more clothes? Is there a general store or something like that around here? I need some toiletries and stuff too."

"Oh my I forgot you basically came here with nothing but that dress." Daria drops the bag on one of the tables near the kitchen and focuses her attention back on me.

"Yeah, I mean the stuff you gave me is great, but I don't want to run through all your clothes especially if it seems like we are going to be stuck here for a while." I hope I didn't hurt her feelings since Daria is one of the sweetest women I have ever met. I didn't want her to think that I was being ungrateful.

"No, I completely understand. You need your own things. I will have Clay run out and pick you up the necessities. Let him know your sizes and he will get you whatever they have." She picks up the bag again and makes her way into the kitchen.

So far, we have a woman named Capri here, Sheeba, Sade, a little boy named Zoomer, an older woman name Lordes, and another older woman named Delia, who they tell me is Pirate's Ol' Lady or was at some point. All of them family members of the Wings of Diablo crew and none of them looking too happy that they have to be stuck here.

I'm ready to just go right back into my room. They must all know that this is because of me. It's embarrassing to be the reason behind all these sour faces.

The roar of bikes sounds from someplace close outside, the noise getting louder until it comes to a stop right outside the front entrance. I look expectantly at the door and pray that it's Jameson and my father. When Clay opens the door and I hear heavy boots tromping over the threshold, I hold my breath in the hope that my father is with one of them. Jameson walks in and closes the door behind him. My head falls and it feels like someone just kicked me in the gut. Tears I didn't realize that I was holding back stream down my face. Before I stumbled onto these guys, my father was all I had. My mother had died when I was young. He did everything he could to make sure that I was raised correctly even though he was nothing but a child himself when he had me. Where is he? My father would never just abandon me, no matter what René said. The fact that we still couldn't find him after so many days since me having run away, it's starting to feel like maybe he truly is dead. Did I kill my father when I escaped?

I heave in a huge breath and turn to the room. I rush in and close the door behind me. No one should see me like this.

I pace back and forth in the small space. Usually this works to calm my brain down, but now it does nothing except get me further worked up. The tears continue to run down my face and I feel my hands begin to shake. It feels like someone has their hand in my gut and is twisting my insides around. All the unknown is wrecking my brain. Having to do all this waiting to see what is going to happen is making me go crazy. I wring my hands together as images of the possible positions or places my father could be dying begin to flash like a movie projector through my head. He could be scared, alone, and in pain.

"Oh God, oh God, oh God." I mutter over and over trying to get the images to leave. I can't focus on that, because if I do, I'll run out of here right now and straight back to René. He would give me to Thomas and then he'd chop my clit off with a nail file or something crazy like that. I'd do it too, if it meant that my dad would be safe.

I hear Jameson before he even gets to the door. I do all that I can to get myself together, but the harder I try to calm down the harder I cry.

It feels like I'm about to break apart at any moment and no matter how hard I try to hold myself together I can feel myself slipping away.

"Shit." Jameson takes one look at me, and my pain is instantly mirrored in his dark whiskey colored eyes.

"Where is he?" I ask out loud. I just want someone to tell me where he is. "Jameson, we should have found him by now.

He strode straight towards me and engulfs me in his large arms. The feel of him holding me up seems to break the final thread of calmness that I have and I wail into his chest. "Shhh … Darlin' don't cry. Please don't cry." His smooth voice now gruff with despair.

"Where is my dad? I just need to know. I need to know if he's ok." I beg him for an answer I know he doesn't have.

He pulls me back slightly holding my face in his hands, gentler than he would hold a new born baby, "Celine, we are going to find him. I swear to you we will. Whatever we find we will get through it together. You hear me? I'm here. I'm not going anywhere. I'm with you." He doesn't wait for me to answer, just pulls me back into his chest and lets me cry my pain away while his worn leather kutte absorbs my river of tears.

CHAPTER 19

JAMESON

It doesn't take Celine long to pull herself together, but seeing her break down like that was almost more than I could take. In the second I'd opened up the door every idea imaginable sprang into my mind as a way to get her father back to her. Even when I was with Monica, I never had the urge to protect someone as completely as I do with Celine. I never want her to cry like that again.

Once she does calm herself down, she goes about helping the Ol' ladies and other family members with what they need. She and Tink do a little cooking. Clay and Mark and a few other patched in members went down to the strip to pick up some clothes for her, so she was happy about that. I have never seen someone get so excited over leggings. I make a mental note to give her a little shopping trip once we come out of lockdown. She should have nice things. With the club doing well in the gambling business I wasn't really hurting for cash. I mean, I couldn't by a house with cash straight out, but I had enough put away that she should be able to go shopping and not worry about how it's going to hit my wallet.

"I'm glad you have her." Archer says from the side of me.

I flinch and have to calm my heart down before I speak to him. Even when we were deployed together this bastard was always sneaking up on me. "What the fuck is that supposed to mean?" I ask him, but don't take offense to what he is saying. Archer has been my closest friend since I was old enough to join the military. If there is anyone that knows me better than I know myself it's him.

"She gives you purpose."

That was not what I was expecting to hear. I turn my eyes on him, wanting to see his expression. It's calm, like always. "Are you saying I didn't have purpose before? I like to think I did my fucking job well." If he says I didn't, I would take offense to that shit.

"Of course, you did. You followed every order, went above and beyond, but Celine gives you a reason to fight besides just us being family. You push harder, because you don't want her to hurt. You don't want her to fear anything. There should always be at least one thing in your life that will have you question a command. Something that forces you to take stock of the decisions that you make and what the reactions will cause. For me it's Daria, and now for you it's Celine. She's given you purpose." He shrugs one shoulder and walks off leaving me there just trying to internalize what he'd just said. There is nothing that would come between me and this club, but he was right when he said that I'm taking care to make better decisions. I want to come back to her.

I scrub my hands up and down my face for a second before I let what Archer said leave my thoughts. It was no use in fighting it now. The girl was deep under my skin.

By the evening, the clubhouse was basically bursting at the seams. Everyone that meant anyone to us that was close enough to get, we brought in. Even Pirate brought in his Ol' lady. They are estranged for now, but the way he looks at her lets me know that he still has love for that woman. I can't say it's the same for her though.

Daria and Tink arranged a small party to take the edge off everyone, there are even a few club bunnies who have been with us from the start that Archer allows to stay. They are going to be playing girlfriend to those who don't have ol' ladies while we are all on lockdown. It takes a little while, but eventually Celine comes out of her shell and falls into her stride when it comes to all the new people. She laughs and drinks with them, listens intently as they tell her stories about their men or family members that have her tossing her head back in joy. Every once in a while, she will look for me, her eyes scanning the room quickly. Sometimes lazily and other times in a panic, but every time she finds me the same look of adoration and lust overtakes her features. I can get used to this for sure.

By midnight, the small party that was going on is coming to an end and Celine is becoming bolder by the second. I sit at the bar with Yang and Shyne, we just observe the crowd in our clubhouse.

"Man, I wish I would have found her in the river and then maybe she would be walking up to me like that." I look over to Shyne who is looking to the side of the room. I swing around in my chair so I can see the what he is talking about.

Celine is walking slowly towards me, her eyes slightly hooded and a half empty glass clenched between her fingers. She stares at me. When she realizes that she has my attention, she bites her bottom lip and uses her free hand to comb her thick long light brown hair to the side so its hanging down over her shoulder.

"You sure you want that one?" Shyne says from behind me. I turn and stare him down.

"I'm only going to say this shit once and if I ever hear anything fucking different, I'll rip your fucking eyes out of your skull, Celine is mine. Stay the fuck off her." Both Shyne and Yang back up in surprise and put their hands up like I had just brandished a gun.

"Damn brother we were just fucking around with you," Shyne is the first one of the two to put his hands down.

"Yeah, I'm not playing with this one, don't fuck around." I turn my eyes back to Celine who is standing right next to me now.

"You going to threaten everyone that looks at me?" She puts the glass down on the counter and then wraps her arms around my neck to play with the locks at the base of my skull. The feeling shoots shivers down my spine.

"Not everyone."

"Jameson, you know this isn't going to work if you don't trust me, right? I mean you are aware that I'm not going to cheat on you."

This isn't the time to have this conversation. I believe that she believes that she will never cheat on me just like I believed that Monica would never cheat on me, but shit changes. I may not be able to control her as completely as I might want to, but I'll be damned sure to let everyone around me know that she is mine. If they try anything after that I won't have a fucking regret in the world when I beat their faces in. My claim on her is their one and only warning.

"I got it Darlin', but these bastards don't have any type of class. If I didn't let them know they would have pressed up on you."

Shyne nods his head and takes a swig of his beer. He knows that I'm speaking nothing but fact, the man is a fucking horn dog. I laugh and she moves in closer to me. When I turn back in her direction, she lays a soft kiss on my lips. Everything around me just fades away and if she didn't move back at that exact moment, I would have ripped her clothes off right there. "I'ma hit the sack, you gonna come lay with me right, when you're done? No rush."

I pull her in for another kiss, I just can't get enough of her. "Yeah, I'll be there."

When she exhales, I realize that she was nervous to ask me that. Not that I fucking understood why, she could ask me to go with her right now and I would rocket the fuck out of my chair. She must not really understand the hold that she has on me. Hell, I don't even fucking understand it.

I watch her as she walks away from me and into the room. I sit with the boys for another few minutes, but for the most part everyone is already off to bed. Thoughts of Celine laying in my bed just waiting for me to come take her keeps me at the edge of my seat. I don't want to come off as a fucking desperate fuck, but I don't want to hold out any longer. I want to go be with my woman.

"Alright fellas, I'm down for the night. Who's guarding the door?"

"It's Mark tonight. I was wondering when you were going to get your head out your ass." Yang said as he stood up from his stool as well.

"What the hell? What does that mean?"

"Bro, she didn't come over here to tell you she was going to go to sleep. That woman was trying to get you to follow her. She probably already started without you."

"What … What's happening? Started? Can I watch?" Shyne, who had fallen asleep with his head on the bar top, woke right up at the sound of that.

"Really?" I ask Yang. It's possible. That's why I fucking told her that

I don't play damn games. It's been too long since I've had to decipher hints and clues from a woman. I just want to know the answers. "Fuck." I hustle in the direction of my room, but I'm a little disappointed to see that she is safely tucked under the covers, both her hands visible. No party's started here.

"You just going to stand there all night and stare at me or are you going to come lay down?" Celine rolls over and her eyes rake over my body as she pulls her bottom lip into her mouth.

"Did you want me to come in here before?" I take my time as I pull my kutte off and hang it on the coat rack over my door. I kick off my shoes and pull my shirt over my head. Once I'm down to only my jeans she still hasn't responded to me.

"Celine, I asked you something Darlin'. Did you want me to come in here with you when you told me that you were going to sleep?"

"Yeah, I mean no. I wasn't going to get mad if you didn't want to. You're grown, your wants are not always going to be the same as mine." Her cheeks blush, but she doesn't turn away.

"What did I tell you about games?"

"I'm not playing any games." She throws the covers off and stands up out of the bed. She is wearing one of my shirts. I was sure that the prospects had got her some night clothes. Based on the bags and bags of shit that they walked in with I'd thought they did. I'm not complaining though. The shirt is big, but it's not very long on her. It stops right at the top of her thighs, rising up even more in the back. My dick stirs to life and quickly stands to attention.

"Celine if you want me in bed just say so. I don't do hints well. I never have. I know you ain't fucking shy so speak your mind in all things when it comes to us."

"I shouldn't have to tell you how to do this." She crosses her arms over her chest and cocks a hip out, always ready to fight.

"Yeah, the fuck you do. If you want something from me, you going to have to ask or you may never get it." I shrug and wait for her to tell me to lay down with her.

She drops her hands to her side, she looks down at the bulge in my pants and swallows a large gulp before looking back up, "Jameson, make me feel like you did before. Kiss me. Touch me." Her voice is soft and unsteady. A pleading look is etched on her face and her hands tremble slightly. She's nervous.

I close the distance between us before I tip her chin upwards, press my lips to hers and let the sparks explode at the edge of each one of my nerves. I wonder if I will ever stop fucking feeling like this. I sip at her lips, barely touching them, trying to memorize every smooth layer of them. She pulls up on her tip toes and tries to deepen the kiss—tries to take over. I grab her hair and yank it back so she is in the position that she was previously in. I wasn't fucking done.

"Jameson." She whimpers when she realizes that I'm not going to let her go. "Please, I don't know how ..." her words cut off and she moans louder as I drop my head down to her neck and trail kisses from there up to her ear.

"You asked for this and I'm going to fucking deliver." I growl in her ear as I lift her so that her legs wrap around my waist.

"Is this really going to happen this time." She laughs, more nervousness, but she raises up to swipe her lips across mine.

"You want it to happen this time?"

"Yes, God yes."

The world could have exploded right then, because nothing else matters now that I have her consent. She wants me and I'm going to give her all of me. I drop her down onto the bed and make quick work of taking her shirt off. I suck and bite at her neck and chest as I fight to unbuckle my pants. I'm moving too fast now, I know I am, but I'm just as needy as she is. My control snapped the second she was underneath me. I should be worshipping her, but I can't focus on that right now. A deeper animalistic need consumes me and all I can think about is emptying my sack inside of her.

I get out of my pants and kick them to the other side of the room. I wrap an arm behind her back and roughly tug her up on the bed so that I can make some room for myself.

"Oh God, Jameson. I want to ... I don't want to wait anymore." She paws at me and I can feel the strength of her tugs, but I can also see the way her body is trembling.

"Darlin' I'm here for you. Just relax. I'm going to give you more than you can fucking handle." I smile at her and kick my boxers off. My cock is hard and a drop of precum is leaking from the tip.

Her face goes even redder than a few seconds ago. I wasn't expecting this reaction. The ladies usually love the size of my cock and I'm used to a bit of excitement, but she looks scared.

"You want me to stop? You have to talk to me Celine." I push her head up so that she is looking at me and not staring wide eyed at my dick.

"No, no, don't stop. I want to. You're just so big. I don't know ..." She doesn't finish her sentence, but she grabs onto me and tries to pull me down again.

"I'll fit." I reply trying to answer her unspoken question. "I fucking promise I'm going to get balls deep inside of you. I want you to feel every inch of me in you."

She groans and her legs get tighter around me. "Now, please, just do it." She pants wildly and uses one of her free hands to pull me down. Our mouths crash together as the intense need to fuck overtakes the both of us.

She raises her hips up and her warm slick entrance just grazes the head of my cock, "Fuck, motherfuck!" I grunt out and my hips slightly buck down without my say so. This feels like a fight for survival, my body is doing what it needs to in order to relieve the tension.

"Oh, please." It sounds like she might cry. Desperate and in agony, she tries to force me inside her again. This time I gather what little wits I have left and snake my hand in between us. My fingers find her tight nub and I rub quickly, using the slick juices coating her cunt to lubricate my movements.

"Oh, oh fuck." She leans up and tries to kiss me, but after the first two kisses she sucks in a breath and just presses her forehead to mine. "I'm coming, I'm going to come." She mumbles and her eyes slam shut.

"Fuck yes, come for me." She is so fucking wet right now that I'm sure she's soaked through my sheets.

Her eyes flutter open as her legs clench hard on my waist. "Oh ... Yessss" She hisses and falls back down to the bed moaning loud.

"You clean Darlin'?" I ask her, I know I should wait. I'm being so fucking selfish right now but I can't help myself.

"Hmm?" She asks her body still trembling hard both from nerves and the orgasm she just had.

"I'm going to fuck you bare, I need to know ..." A deep grumble settles deep in my throat as my hips dip down once again all on their own and I can basically feel her heat welcoming me in.

"I've never, never, never ... I trust you. Yes, I trust you." She pulls at me again, clearly that one orgasm wasn't enough to satiate her. She trusts me and even though I've never found myself so convinced about someone so quickly, I know that I trust her too. Un-fucking-conditionally.

I feel myself mentally let go, there's no need to hold back now. I swipe my cock against her pussy once to soak myself with her cum and then I dive straight into her.

"Ahhh!" She screams out when I enter her.

"Fuck!" I bark out at the same second. I drop my head down to her neck so that my face is hidden from her gaze. I don't want her to see me breaking apart like a wuss. She is so fucking tight, almost painfully tight, I'm not going to last more than a few pumps. I don't think I've ever been in a pussy this fucking tight. I want to live and die here.

"Celine, you're fucking perfect." I groan into her ear as I continue to thrust into her making sure to get as deep as possible and grind into her as hard as I can. I kiss on her neck, but it's only then that I realize she isn't responding to anything that I'm doing. In fact, her hands have latched onto the covers under us and she is barely moaning anymore. It's been a while, but I didn't think I had lost all my fucking mojo.

"Darlin'?" I raise my head up and see that she is more than just uncomfortable, the woman is in pain. Her eyes are tightly squeezed shut and her lips pressed into a thin line. Fuck I'm really hurting her. I know there are some guys that get off on that, but I'm not one of them. I want to see her struggling with how much she is enjoying my cock, not struggling in pain.

"Celine! You ok? I'm sorry I'm stopping."

"No, just keep going, I'm fine." She says through gritted teeth, but she still hasn't opened her eyes.

"Open your eyes."

"Jameson, please, just go on. I'm fine." She says again and takes a deep breath.

"Open your fucking eyes!" I roar down at her. This shit is not going like I had thought it was going to go. My cock is still buried deep inside of her, but I can feel myself starting to get soft.

She exhales roughly and opens her eyes slowly, then blinks quickly trying to get her vision to refocus.

Her eyes dart over my shoulder. The blush that colors her face drains away as she starts screaming and pushing me away. I turn my head slightly and the shiny silver metal of a gun is the first thing I see.

CHAPTER 20

JAMESON

"What the fuck!"

The world comes rushing back to me in an instant. I pull out of Celine and she skitters backwards. I have to protect her. I can't lose her. I can't.

Rage, pure white hot rage erupts inside of me when I get a glimpse of who the hell is holding a gun on me.

This bitch.

"You fucking homewrecker! That was the worst fucking I've ever seen in my life. You gave me up for that shit? You can't just fucking toss me away like that Jam!" Monica screams at Celine who is pressed up against the headboard with the edge of the covers pulled up over her naked body.

"Are you out of your fucking mind?" I roar loud enough to shake the fucking windows.

"Jam don't scream at me. I should fucking kill her for what you're doing to me. You told me you fucking loved me, Jameson!" Monica whines and stomps her foot.

I can disarm her. I don't have a problem doing it, but the gun she is holding is mine and I know it's loaded. I don't want to lunge for her and have it go off. It could hurt Celine.

"Monica, put the motherfucking gun down." I speak clearly.

"No! I won't ... I hate her. She can't even fuck you like I can. You're mine, Jam. I fucked up and I'm sorry. How long are you going to keep punishing me?" She screeches and then focuses her attention back on

Celine. "You fucking club bunny whore, stay the fuck away from my man!"

"If I'd known he was your fucking man, I wouldn't be here." Celine barks back.

"Bitch, who the fuck do you think you are talking to? I will blow a fucking hole in your chest. My man got my back, they will never fucking find your body."

I feel like my head is swiveling around like the fucking exorcist. What man is she talking about?

"I'm talking to you, bitch. The only reason your ass isn't knocked the fuck out right now is because you got that gun pointed at me. Put that shit down and then come try me." Celine stares her down. "That's my bad on fucking your man, he caught me up."

"What the fuck are you talking about? You know motherfucking well that I'm not with her." I finally am able to speak up.

"She's got a gun pointed at me. Jameson, looks like ya'll are still working shit out." Her words drip with acid as she rolls her eyes and looks away from me.

"Oh what the fuck, who let this bitch in here?" Pirate is standing at my door with his sweat pants on and nothing else.

Monica turns her head at the sound of his voice and that is the only opening that I need. I jump out of the bed and push the gun up over her head. I grab her face and squeeze hard.

"Let fucking go now!" My voice booms through the room and she cringes slightly, but immediately lets go of the gun. I put my piece back on the side table where I always leave it.

I can't believe I was so fucking gone that I didn't hear her come in. If she was any more of a crazy bitch, Celine or I would be dead.

"No wonder you strayed with this bitch, what kind of kinky shit are you in to?" Monica laughs before she sniffles and wipes more tears off her face.

"What?" I turn to look at her.

"This bitch let you cut her, that's what you like? You want to see blood now?" She squints her eyes at me before she lets them drag down my naked body.

Blood? What blood?

"Oh shit." Pirate says his eyes wide before he turns around and walks away, "I'm getting Daria." He shouts back.

I look down at myself.

"What in the fuck!" My cock, my lower abdomen, and even the top of my thighs are sticky with smears of blood. I look at the bed and there are two half dollar sized drops of bright red blood. I quickly grab myself and figure out the blood isn't mine.

Celine.

Oh God, what did I fucking do?

"Oh fuck, Celine! You're hurt. Shit." I charge the bed and try to get to her. I was too fucking rough. She's bleeding internally. Fuck.

"No!" She jumps out of the bed before I can touch her and I can see there is one small drop of blood rolling down her leg. "Don't touch me, I'm fine." She glares at me.

How the fuck can she say that she is fine? Granted she doesn't look like she is in much pain, but there's blood.

"Oh, you sneaky bitch." Monica charges again and I have to turn to catch her before she gets to Celine. "You really thought if you let him pop your cherry, you'd be more than just a 2 dollar slut!"

Oh.

Fuck.

No.

The pin drops in my head and I replay everything that had happened. She was so tight, her nervousness, the uncertainty. Celine was a virgin and I had just fucked her like a goddamn savage.

"Shut the fuck up, Monica!" I shake her hard almost willing for her head to pop off her shoulders.

"Fuck this." Celine wraps herself up in the sheet and walks wide around the both of us.

"Where in the fuck are you going?" I turn to try and catch her, but I can't let go of Monica.

"This not the drama I signed up for. Go be with your woman. You don't have to fucking worry about me anymore." She spat out before she rushes out and into her room.

"Son of a bitch!" I scream at the top of my lungs and I see Daria's head pop in my room, her doe eyes wide and searching.

"Don't let her leave! You hear me Daria. Don't let her go." A few seconds after I give that order I see Celine walking by fully clothed with a bag over her shoulder.

"Wait, Celine! You don't understand. Just give him a second." Daria runs behind her.

"Look, now we're even, ok. We can finally get past this." Monica stops squirming in my arms and tries to wrap her arms around my neck. I grab her hand and bend it back, "Ow, Jam, you're hurting me!" She cries and a fresh set of tears springs to her eyes. I want to rip her fucking hand off. I want to grab the back of her head and slam it through the steel and wood wall of the clubhouse. She probably just ruined the one chance I had at being with someone I truly fucking cared about and she was talking about how we could finally move past her fuck up.

"Jameson, that's a woman. I know she's a bitch, but that's still a woman." Yang is standing at my door, he must see how close I am to beating the shit out of her.

I let her hand go and she quickly cradles it to her chest, "Get the fuck out." My voice is low, but I know she heard me.

"Jameson, just let me ..."

"Now! Get the fuck away from me now!" I roar, my chest heaves up and down with deep breaths that I'm forcing myself to take.

"Let's go, Monica." Yang steps up and pulls Monica by the arm. She reaches out for me and I have to restrain myself from slapping her hand.

Once she is out of the room, I pace back and forth, and shove my hands into my hair. I tug at the strands hard to try and come to grips with what the fuck had just happened.

Celine was a virgin? How in the fuck is that possible and why didn't she tell me? How the fuck did Monica even get in here? I'm murderous and pissed off, but mostly I'm fucking scared. Celine could fucking decide right now that she wants nothing to do with me and I won't be able to blame her. Not only did I fuck up her first time, but her first ever experience with sex was traumatizing with a fucking gun to her head. I had no idea how the hell I was going to fix this or even if she was going to let me.

I don't have time to think about it anymore. I have to make moves. I rush over to the bathroom and wipe myself down quickly before I grab some sweats and a Henley to throw on. I shove my feet into my shit kickers and tear out of my room. The door slams open so hard one of the hinges pops clear off.

"Get the hell off me! You want me to knock you out again!" Celine squirms and kicks as Pirate has her in a bear hug.

"Celine, please just let him get this under control before you leave." Daria is still right there trying to get her to listen.

"She's not fucking going anywhere." I snap at the three of them.

Celine stops fighting Pirate and her eyes darken with fury as she glares at me. "Who the fuck do you think you are? Where the hell do you get off thinking you can tell me anything?"

"I know who the fuck I am, and I know who the fuck you are. My woman. I got shit to handle with this cunt over here," I fling a thumb in the direction of the door, "When she's gone, which will be very soon, you are going to explain why the fuck you didn't tell me some important shit. I told you I don't play fucking games and I told you to be sure you really wanted to be mine. You said you did, you don't get to just walk the fuck out. This isn't over. You want to be mad? You want to fight? I can take it, all of it. We can do all that shit, but you're gonna do it in my goddamn bedroom. Now cut the shit and go put your bags down."

With every word that came out of my mouth her eyes and mouth opened wider and wider. Until she was standing there gaping like a fish, searching for something to say that would counteract my audacity. She chuckles in disbelief and then shakes her head again completely bewildered. I made sure to not break my gaze with her. I couldn't show any weakness right now or she would pounce all over that shit. I know her too well already. If she feels like she has the upper hand she will keep on pushing.

"I'm not staying, but I'll wait until she leaves." She cuts her eyes at me and then simply walks back into my bedroom, closing the busted door as best she can.

I nearly thank the Lord out loud when she doesn't try to run. I turn my attention towards the door, I can still hear Monica acting up outside.

There is someone else out there though, who I want to beat the shit out of. Luckily for me, he's a man and a prospect. Finally someone I can lay hands on.

I rush towards the door and before he can move, I have Mark up by his prospect rags against the door. "You fucking no good piece of shit." I slam him hard against the door and the few photos that are hanging nearby rattle with the force.

"Jameson, what did I do?"

"Keep on acting fucking stupid, you know exactly what the fuck you did." I snarl at him before I let him down, but I don't back out of his face. I want him to say something disrespectful so I can throw his ass through the fucking window.

"I don't. I didn't sleep, stayed at my post. I don't know what I did." Mark fell into his ingrained stance, feet shoulder width apart, hands behind the back, back and neck straight, eyes averted over my shoulder—the perfect fucking solider.

"Why the fuck did you let her in?"

His eyes dart to me, "Ya'll told me to. You told me to let all the family in. You married her, didn't you? She's still a part of your family." Mark stares at me a second longer before he averts his eyes back to the wall behind me.

"You calling a vote for this?" Archer asks. Everyone is out of their rooms now with all the fucking commotion going on. Archer wants to know if I'm going to vote that Mark not continue with his term as prospect.

It would be easy. All I would have to do is say yes and Mark would be on his way. I won't though. He's not wrong. She may be fucked up in the head, but she is still a part of my family. A part I wished I could shove deep into the earth where no one would ever find it, but still a fucking part of it none the less.

"Nah." I back up slightly and Mark falls out of his tense stance. "For the record," I raise my voice loud enough for everyone in the clubhouse to hear me. "Monica is not to set foot inside these walls without my explicit consent or there's dire fucking circumstances and even then, she doesn't move past the bar. Everyone got it?" I turn back to Mark and he nods his head yes. I don't wait for anyone else to answer since they all know the deal, at least now they do. I push past Mark and get outside to see Monica is still there pacing back and forth cursing at the wind.

"I'm going to tell you this one last fucking time." I don't wait for her to realize that I'm there with her before I go in on her, "We are not together, you're not my woman. I don't want you and in no time in the future will I ever want you back."

"Jam, how can you be so mean? You don't mean that."

"What the fuck do I have to say Monica? What do I have to do for you to get it through your head? I don't love you. In fact, I can't stand to look at you. I deal with you, because we have history. But even that shit is starting to wear fucking thin."

"What does she have that I don't?"

"Morals, backbone, closed legs." I rattle the list off immediately.

"You're never going to forgive me, are you?" She drops her head. Even though I know it can all be a play to get me to admit that I have some phantom feelings for her it does look like she is really hurting.

"Monica, I already forgave you. You're forgiven. Parts of me doesn't even fucking blame you for how shit went down, but I don't trust you. I'm never going to trust you. You have to accept that shit and move on. Learn from our mistakes and find another man who is going to give you what you need. It's not me. I promise you it's not."

When a blank look crosses her face, I have hope that her tirade is all but finished, "You in love with her?"

"I'm getting there." I say with no hesitation. It's been nothing, but a fucking whirlwind since I met Celine. Yet, if there is one thing I'm sure of it's that I want to be with her.

"I hope she can handle you." Monica sniffles again and wraps her arms around herself.

"I hope so too." I roll my eyes and pull her into a hug, but make sure she doesn't get a chance to move her arms around me. She might be a good woman, she's just not my woman.

"I'm going to leave. I don't think I can stay in the same space as the two of you." She mutters against my chest.

"Where you want to go?"

"Up, I was thinking Maine. Try and get a fresh start."

"What you need?"

"You." She raises her eyes to me, still hopeful.

"Not going to happen Monica." I roll my eyes and pull away from her.

"Yeah, I got it." She lets out a sigh, "You have a few dollars you can lend me. I'll pay you back when I get settled?"

Money? That shit I could do.

"Hold on." I turn away from her and walk over to the door. Mark opens it right away, ready to do whatever I need.

"Yeah, Jameson?"

"Go get my bug out case from Archer. He knows what it is. Get it fast." The longer I am out here with Monica the more time Celine has inside to figure out a way to leave me.

Mark takes off and a minute later comes back with a shoe box sized plastic container.

Inside of it is my passport along with two fakes, a gun, keys to a bike I keep hidden and cash—twenty thousand dollars to be exact. I take half of it and give it to her. Ten thousand is nothing if it keeps her safe and away from me.

"Wait, this is too much." She smiles wide but tries to give me some of it back.

"Monica, take it all. If you're serious about all the shit that you just said, then you are going to need it. I'll make it back."

"Thanks Jam." She takes the money and starts towards her car. "Can I offer some advice?"

"No." I shake my head she has no place interjecting her thoughts about Celine and I knew that is where she was going.

"Jameson, I'm still a woman."

"Fine, what?"

"Well, her first time will probably be the worst she'll ever have so make sure you show her the very best. You won't erase her first time, but you can spend every time after that making it up to her. Good luck." She grins at me before she opens her car door and gets inside. I barely wait until she pulls out of the small driveway before I'm running back inside.

I shove my bug out box back into Mark's arms. "Give this back to Archer and don't let anyone into my goddamn room."

Again, I don't wait for an answer. I have a woman to fight with and I can't fucking wait.

CHAPTER

21

CELINE

I can't fucking believe I let myself get so caught up in everything that is going on. This is why I never had sex before. I don't have time for this shit and don't want to deal with it. I just want to find my father, stay the hell away from Thomas and live my life in peace.

I exhale hard and let my head fall back. I pace back and forth in the room, my knee still a bit achy from the other night. Despite that it's the pain in my upper thighs that has me moving slowly.

I don't know why I didn't tell him. I didn't think it would be a big deal and honestly now that I've experienced sex I don't understand what all the craziness is about. The anticipation far outweighed the actual act and it was just painful.

I have a good mind to never do it again. I've gone twenty-three years prior to this without having sex, I think I can put it off for another twenty-three.

I hear the door to the front open and close, then Jameson's smooth voice still heavy with anger tells that poor prospect something. Then quick footsteps follow. I stand tall and wait for him to open the door. I might as well get this over with now.

The door opens and he roots me to the spot with his glare. I almost lose my shit right there. What the fuck, he has the nerve to be mad at me.

"Jameson, I'm telling you right now fix the attitude, because I'm not going to stand for it. You have no right to be mad at me. It's your wife that caught us in bed together."

"Ex-wife." He snaps, "She's my ex-wife and you already knew that."

"So what the hell is up with the death glare?"

He relaxes his stance slightly before he walks over to where I am. He grabs my face, but not hard like I was expecting.

"Darlin' why didn't you tell me?" his voice is like velvet wrapping me in a cocoon. I don't want it to affect me, especially after what I know sex is like now, but just those few words have me squeezing my thighs together in need.

"There was nothing to tell." I shrug and try to pull away from him.

"Celine, don't fucking lie to me. How the hell can I trust you when you hide something that huge from me?"

"I wasn't hiding it. I wasn't ... I just didn't know how to say it. I mean it's not the norm." I look away from him. "What does it matter anyway?"

Now it's his turn to pull away, "Are you kidding? It would have made a world of difference. You shouldn't lose your virginity like that. Ravaged like a beast. I would have taken my time, or at least I would have tried. I would have prepared you more. I would have gone easy."

All of that sounds very mechanical, like there is a play book that he would have followed for my first time. Why the hell would I want that? "I wanted you, right then, I didn't want to wait for the right time. That was the right time and the right way. It just wasn't what I was expecting ... during or after."

"I want you now." His voice is nothing more than a groan as he moves in closer to me, his lips inching towards mine.

I sigh and feel my core contract deliciously.

No, he has a wife!

My subconscious screams at me and I shake myself from his spell, "What the hell do you think you are doing? You're woman ..."

"Fix that shit!" Jameson barks out and it startles me so much that I jump.

"Chill out, fine. Your ex-wife came in here with a gun. She wants to kill me. I don't want to deal with that mess, Jameson. A jealous boyfriend I can deal with, a crazy jealous ex-wife I cannot."

"You don't ever have to deal with her again." He looks away and then looks back at me, "That's a lie. Mark let her in the clubhouse, which everyone knows not to do. But he let her in, because he was told to let all the family in. I may not want anything to do with her, but she was my wife for a period of time. I have some level of responsibility to her so you may see her again, but I told her under no circumstance were me and her ever getting back together. I will never trust her and I can't be with someone I don't trust. She's had a hard fucking time getting that shit through her head, but I think she finally did."

What makes this time any different than the others? What is stopping her from showing up tomorrow trying to get back in his life? "Why do you think that?"

"She's moving. She said that she wants to start some place new, get a fresh start and all that shit. She was looking to go up to Maine, that is a hell of a distance."

Maine? Oh shit, "Well damn, that is going to make it hard for her to just pop in on you." I laugh and he takes that moment to step in closer to me.

"You going to be honest with me now?"

"Depends on what you ask?" I don't want to be this easy. I should be stark raving mad right now, but just him holding me like this has my heart doing flips in my chest. Motherfucking hormones.

"Did you enjoy yourself at all?"

Oh crap, we're going to talk about it. Can't we just sweep it under the rug? Let him have another notch on his belt and I can finally say I'm no longer a virgin.

"Yeah. I did." I smile and he tightens his grip on my waist, but not in a good way. "Fine, no. I didn't. After you made me come it was all kind of downhill from there." I bite my lip and try to gauge his reaction. I have never heard of a man who's ever wanted to hear that they were bad in bed. It was a whole thing back in high school, one rumor that you were bad in the sack and that could mean you were no longer one of the popular crew.

"How much pain are you in right now?"

"What?" I wasn't expecting that.

"Inside, are you hurting? I was really rough with you, Darlin'. I wish I hadn't been, but we can't change that now. I need to know how bad you are hurting." He ran his hands up and down my arms causing goosebumps to erupt on my skin.

"It isn't as bad as it was when it was happening. I'm ok." I whisper and my mouth moves closer to his. Why the fuck do I still want to do this, I know what happens. I feel like a dumb ass for going back down this road.

I let my tongue come out to trace the edge of his bottom lip and he tugs me against him hard. "You see, that shit right there, that's how I lost my head the first time." He takes a step back and I feel almost bereft.

I pout, but try to shake the face off when I catch him smiling at me. "It's ok. I guess we should chill out anyway."

"Chill out, oh no Darlin' … I'm not going to let you chill out. I am just going to take my time with you and you are going to sit back and enjoy every fucking second of it." He leans forward again and picks me up like a bride.

I squeal at the sudden motion, "What the heck, Jameson, what are you doing?"

"Hush, woman. Let me take care of you." He grunts as we make our way into the bathroom.

Oh yeah, I'm still bloody. "I can take care of this part, you don't need to do this."

"Did I fucking ask you if I needed to do this? I want to fucking do it." He turns on the shower and lets the water run while he quickly sheds his clothing. He still has a few spots of blood on him.

"Sorry about that, and your sheets. I'll get you some new ones."

He quickly turns me around so that I'm facing the mirror and pulls my head to the side, "Don't you fucking apologize for that. That blood is proof that I'm the first one to ever take you. The first one to ever claim every piece of you. If I could hang those sheets in a fucking frame I would. By the time I'm done with you, your cunt will be a perfect mold for my dick." He snags my ear and a shiver runs down my spine.

"Oh fuck it. I'll give it another go." I spin quickly in his arms and press my mouth to his.

He laughs loud before he kisses me back. His hands pull up the shirt that I'm wearing and his fingers tweak and pull on my nipples.

"Jameson, I like that." I whisper.

"Yes, that's right tell me what the fuck drives you wild so I can do that shit just how you like it all the time." He switches to the other side and does the same motion. I push myself as close to him as I can get and feel his hard cock through his sweats. I already know first-hand that he is huge. It still scares me, but I want to see if I can take it on— my very own personal challenge!

I lift my leg up and hook it on his thigh trying to get closer. I cringe slightly as the ache radiates through my legs.

"Stop it." He orders before he finishes taking off my clothes. Apparently, I'm not allowed to be in control today, not that I was in control any other time. He picks me up and settles me in the shower. "Fuck, you are so damn beautiful. Every time I think I get over it you amaze me again." He pushes some of my hair from the side of my face. The water and steam already doing a good job of making my body relax.

He reaches over and grabs a washcloth that he has hanging on one of the rails.

He uses a bit of clear liquid soap. I don't smell anything, so I know it's not scented or anything like that. He lathers it up and begins to wash my body.

"Jameson, I swear, I'm ok. I can do this."

"I'm doing it."

We don't kiss, barely even touch, he just stares at me. I watch a myriad of emotions appearing and disappearing in those intense brown eyes of his. This is almost as bad as me needing him to be inside me. It's so fucking intimate, so exposing that I want to cover myself up. Except I know that there is no amount of clothing that I could put on that would stop him from seeing what he sees in me.

"Don't keep things from me." He grumbles.

"Don't hurt me." I retort right away.

A sly smirk raises one half of his mouth, "Oh Darlin', I can't promise you that. When you aren't so sore, I plan to hurt you a lot and you're going to love every second of it."

I raise up on my tiptoes—a dare. I don't push or pull, just wait. He tries to keep away, but he loses that battle quickly. All this time I thought that I was fighting him for control, trying to be the one in the lead. I was always the one in the lead. I guess they are right when they say pussy rules the world. I'm sure that I could make him do whatever I wanted right now if I just dangle what I have waiting for him between my legs in front of his eyes.

He pulls away from the kiss and turns his head to the side. "Fuck Celine, stop it." he growls.

After he is finished washing my body, he opens one of the cupboard drawers that is right outside the shower and pulls out a fresh washcloth. It looks as if it is made of a softer material. He wets it and softly spreads my legs open. My cheeks heat up with blush as he gently washes my pussy. It's tender, but not unbearably so. What's unbearable is the way he appears to be purposefully avoiding my clit. The different feel of the fabric and his touch drive me wild. I try to move so that he is where I want him to be, but he doesn't let me.

"Jameson, please. I want to try again." I tell him.

"Me too, but this time I want to see you break to pieces in every possible way. First on my face." He pushes me back against the wall of the shower, now the spray of the water hitting him on the back instead of me. "Tell me Darlin' have you ever cum on someone's face before?"

I hadn't since I'd never gotten that far. I shake my head no.

"I'll be the first to taste you. I can't even fucking describe how much of a fucking turn on that is to me." He presses his large, hard body against mine so that I'm flush against him and his cock is pressing against my lower abs. He finds my neck and starts to kiss me there.

"Jameson, you're driving me crazy."

"I know, that's my job." He begins making his way down my body taking a moment or two to kiss and lick up the water that is rolling down my skin. When he makes it down to my legs, he kneels in front of me like he is worshipping a goddess. He looks up at me and my heart clenches in my chest.

"You are the only one to ever bring me to my fucking knees. I hope you respect that shit." The beads of water reflect the lights that are on in the bathroom and cause his eyelashes to become more pronounced. He's beautiful.

I nod, the only response I can muster. He picks up one leg, softly kissing up my calf and thigh before he places my foot on the edge of the shower, splaying my pussy open so he can get to it easily.

"You'll tell me if this gets to be too much."

"Yes, I promise. I'll tell you." I don't want him to think about hurting me or doing anything else right now besides make me feel good.

He kisses me one time and it feels like my legs turn to jelly. Why the fuck is this so intense so quickly? I just couldn't understand how my body could react so completely to just that one small kiss. He presses his hand to my stomach to keep me upright and then he softly begins to lick and suck at my pussy.

"Oh God." I moan and let my head lean back against the wet shower wall. I reach out to the sides trying to find something to help keep me up. There is no way that I'm going to be able to stay like this for long. It feels too good.

My hand instinctively falls down to his head and I grip into his hair. I look down to see if I can tell what he is doing, because every swipe of his tongue has me feeling like all the nerve endings in my body are being tied in knots. The tension and need are so unique. He tilts his head back slightly and his eyes focus in on mine.

"Holy fuck! My God. Jameson. Please. Oh ... Oh." I cry out and try to keep my attention on him, but the feeling of falling is too intense. My legs tremble, any fucking second now I'm going to land flat on my ass and he is going to have to pick me up. His tongue swirls faster and faster. The tip of his tongue now pointed and hard. He flicks my tight nub until I can feel myself start to float and only my grip on Jameson's hair is keeping me attached to the ground.

"Jameson!" I scream as he sucks at my pussy effectively throwing me off the cliff into the intense waves of my climax. My knees buckle, but his one hand is still holding me up. He doesn't stop his assault as my cunt contracts with my pleasure. I want more. I want so much more of that. "Oh God, I can't take it. Too much." I whimper. My legs hurt from the trembling and my core hurts from all the contractions. If I could cry right now it would be from pleasure overload.

He looks at me again and slows his tongue down. He tenderly

kisses the insides of both my legs and gently puts my leg back down so that I'm standing on my own two feet. Barely. "You good Darlin'?

"Hmm? Yes." I answer softly, but I'm honestly worried that I might fall asleep right here on the wall. I just need a little nap.

I feel him take a step back from me and my sleepy eyes follow him until he steps back into the full spray of the shower. He tilts his head back and my body is completely awake now. The water cascades down his body as he rinses off his face and hair. The rivulets of water travel down each crevice of his muscle laced midsection before they roll down his intimidating cock. He looks so powerful standing there like that. Completely unaware of how much I need him and how much he can control me in his own way. He told me that I was the first woman to ever get him on his knees, I want him to be the first man to get me on mine.

I take an uneasy step forward and his eyes pop open. He puts his head forward and a lock of his hair falls forward into his face. It's not long enough to cover his eyes, but still long enough that he has to comb it back.

"Help me." I say and grab onto his biceps. He holds me, but isn't sure of what I need help with. I lower myself to the floor of the shower and I feel him trying to lift me up.

"Celine, no. This is about you today. We can do that another time."

I look up at him through my lashes. "Is this about me?" I question.

"Yeah."

"I want to do this, help me please you Jameson. " I whisper and he groans in need as he wraps his large hand around the shaft of his cock.

"Do whatever the fuck you want. Fucking hell, you're going to make me cum just kneeling there like that. Anything you want to do is perfect." He grunts out.

Of course, I've seen movies and such about people who give head, but I've never done it myself. I guess I never really thought about how much of life I wasn't experienced with. I trusted him to let me know if I was doing something wrong though. I held my hand over his as best I could and did the first thing that I could think to do. I flattened my tongue and licked the underside of the head of his cock to the very tip.

"Oh fuck!" He groans and tries to pull away—sensitive. I open my mouth and suck in that entire section. It's wide and I really have to work my jaw open to get it all in.

I suck a few times and bit of salty liquid splashes on my tongue. "Celine, fuck. Can you take more of me in? Can you try?" He moves his hand and I realize there is at least a good 7 more inches of cock for me to explore. I'm not one to shirk from a challenge so I press my mouth forward and let his dick slide to the top of my throat. I see the muscles in his thighs clenching and releasing with every pump of my mouth. "Shit." He hisses out when I move my tongue. I do it again and he moans even louder. His vocal cues are all I need to keep going. I take a chance and look up at him. He looks desperate and I begin to wonder if I'm hurting him. When I pull back, he grabs my head softly.

"No fuck, don't stop. Keep going." He moans and the sound seems to vibrate deep inside my core. The tightness that I thought would only be brought on by him touching me begins to take hold again. His voice, his need, his desperation for me is winding me up. My hand moves on its own. I find my nipple and begin to knead it, pulling the same way that he did moments before.

His eyes find my hands and his mouth opens softly before his eyes close, "Goddamn it, Celine." He growls as he tightens his grip in my hair. I push him back deeper in my throat. I move faster and more of the salty liquid drops into my mouth.

I tug hard on my nipple and the pain that comes along with it isn't enough to make me stop, but instead drives me further, "MMM." I moan and somehow manage to take more of him into my throat.

"Fuck yes Darlin', show me how much you like this shit." He tugs my head further into his groin and I have to focus on what I'm doing to get him deeper. "Oh shit, how far ... How far can you go?" He pushes my head more and I feel the thick pliable head of his dick curve and try to force its way down my throat. I can't breathe, but I don't want to stop. He holds his breath and pushes in further. Finally, when I can't take it anymore and feel like I might throw up I push away hard and a loud gagging sound comes out of my mouth.

"Fuck, do that again. Come back." He begs and I can see his composure hanging on by just a thread. Jameson is about to lose it and I can't wait to see that.

I rush back to his dick and do the same thing I just did before. This time I catch the rhythm and figure out how to breathe through my nose when he pulls back. He moans and says my name like it's a fucking prayer. This power feels so heavy. He slams his hand against the wall of the shower before he abruptly tugs his cock from my mouth. He squeezes it hard, but doesn't move his hand. I reach for him, but he just moves away.

"No!" He grabs me by the arm and yanks me to my feet. I slide precariously as he attacks me with his mouth. The kisses are no longer slow and planned. These are raw and primal. I struggle to catch my breath between him biting my lips and his tongue plunging deep in my mouth. "Why can't I fucking control myself around you? Shit I don't want to hurt you anymore. My God, I fucking need you." He tugs and pulls at me; all I can do is nod. I want him too, even if it's just to make him feel good, I want him.

"Hold on." He picks me up and quickly moves out of the bathroom not even bothering to turn the water off in the shower. We make it back into his bedroom and he drops me back on the bed. The sheets are still there, my blood has dried, but it doesn't seem to faze him. Our skin is still slick from the water of the shower. His hands rub down the sides of my body and I do my best to relax. Though the nerves that I had before start to pop back up. This is where it all went to shit the last time. This round I'm more prepared though. I know the pain and I'm ready for it.

"No Darlin' keep your eyes open." He orders me and I do just that. He kisses my cheeks, my eyes, and my lips as he lets one of his hands trail down my body. "Tell me if you need me to stop."

"I'm ok." I promise him and my hips settle deeper into the firm mattress. His fingers softly caress my pussy, moving in a circular motion and my back arches. This I like, this man's hands are fucking magical.

"Yes, Jameson. I love it." I murmur as my eyes slowly begin to close.

"You ready for more." His hands move faster and I'm so close to coming. I'm sure that I would tell him anything if he will just get me back to that sweet release.

"More, yes, more."

He removes his hand for the briefest of seconds. Just as I open my mouth to complain I feel one of his fingers slowly press into me. I close my eyes tight trying to bear against the pain I know is sure to come. He moves ever so slowly.

"Talk to me Celine, is it too much?" His face is close to mine. I open one eye and then the other.

"Oh, no. It's ok." I was so surprised that I didn't feel intense pain that I almost laughed. Logically I knew that I could only lose my virginity once. The first time was supposed to be the hardest, but I thought for sure something as intrusive as having a body part shoved up my pussy would always be incredibly painful.

"You have to relax, don't wait for me to hurt you." He kisses me tenderly, "At least not this time."

I smirk and let him have his way with me. He pumps his one finger in and out of me. Instead of the uncomfortable pain, the ache deep inside of me feels different. I want more of it.

"Oh fuck." My hips roll in time with the pump of his hand. He's going to make me come this way too. "Yes, I want more. Please Jameson." He pumps harder into me only stopping once to slip another finger inside of me. I scream out and my body arches off the bed. It's painful, but the consuming pleasure is much more intense.

"Tell me Darlin'." His gravelly voice makes me shiver.

"I'm ...Oh God ... I love it." I mutter and grip his shoulder. "Please, I want you inside of me." If two fingers feel this good, I wonder if his cock will feel better this time around too.

"Please." I beg again, but he moves his hand faster. His fingers moving in a different angle and lights explode behind my eyelids. My back pulls up hard as another orgasm seizes my ability to breathe or even stay still. "Oh God, Jameson!" I scream loud, as my body clenches hard around his fingers and tries to get him deeper inside of me. He pulls away and I scramble for him. "Please, please, please." I need to feel him now. Something about the intensity of these climaxes leaves me feeling so vulnerable. I want him closer.

"Fuck, I hope this is ok." He second guesses himself and quickly shuffles to hover over me. His dick is much bigger than even the two fingers so when he presses the tip of his cock to my already sore flesh I flinch away.

"Darlin' don't do this just for me. I want you to enjoy this. I can wait. I'll die over and over again, but I can wait."

"No, I'm ok. You're so fucking big. I just need to get used to you. Try, please." I look deep in his eyes and I can see the uncertainty, "For me, please. I need you." I scratch my nails against his back and try to pull him down again.

"Dammit, I can't say no. I fucking should." He holds on to his cock and lines it up with my opening. He presses forward slowly and the large head pushes against my slick tender flesh. I hiss, but hold onto his arms pulling him forward more. When he finally pushes past that initial barrier my body begins to open up for him.

"So tight." His arms shake as he struggles to restrain himself.

"More."

He moves in a bit more, pushing my insides apart. Every part of him rubbing against all the parts of me making me purr like a cat.

"I need to fucking move." He grunts and squeezes my thigh. He doesn't though. He is still trying to hold back.

I don't want him to. I roll my hips upwards and take in a bit more of him before I let them fall back down.

"Uhhh, fuck." That one motion kickstarts him into moving. The thrusts are short and soft, but with every one of them I can feel myself wanting to take more.

"Jameson, I can take it. I like it, please give me more." I press on his lower back. This time on his thrust, instead of quickly pulling back so he stays shallow, he presses himself deep. Slowly, mind numbingly slow he impales me with all of his cock.

My teeth chatter at the fullness. "Fuck."

"You good?"

"No." I groan.

"Shit." he tries to pull out, but I lock a leg behind his.

"Jameson, please fuck me. You're killing me." I growl, the need to release is suffocating.

A deep growl rumbles in his chest as he pulls back and thrusts against me. I meet his hips with mine and he thrusts again. "You want me to fuck you, I can do that." He grips my waist and picks up his pace.

The slap of skin is music to my ears as he plunges back and forth into me. Something is still not right though, it's not enough.

"Harder, Jameson. Please."

"Uhhh." He moans and his head falls back as he really starts to pick up speed and strength. "Come, I want you to fucking come on my dick. So fucking tight. I'm not going to last. Perfect." He grits out as his arms work double time to keep the pace. I can feel my orgasm right there just out of reach. With every other stroke he hits something in me that pushes it to the front, but then it moves away. If I could just figure out how to get him to keep hitting that spot, I'd be flying in an instant. I try to lift my hips and find the spot instantly.

"Oh, there!" I call out, but I can't keep my body up. I whimper in defeat when I fall back down and try again to move myself back up.

"I got you baby, I hear you." Jameson pauses and reaches behind me to pull one of the pillows from the top of the bed. He folds it up and lifts me quickly to shove it under me. The confusion as to why he would do that briefly flits through my mind until he lays me back down and begins to pump into me again.

I suck in a deep breath at the intensity, he's got me at the perfect spot and there is no getting away from the pleasure now. "Oh fuck, yes! I'm right there. Right there." I speak gibberish and pull him close to me. He lays his forehead against mine and pumps hard into me.

"Come now." He growls out.

"Oh God." my eyes roll back at the strength and need in his voice. My body falls gloriously into my orgasm and I feel my pussy squeezing his dick tightly.

"Fuck, yes Celine!" He picks up both my legs, hooking his elbows under my knees and thrusts himself over and over into me.

"My God! Jameson!" I cry out. Just as my body tries to complete the round of contractions, I feel myself start to build back up again. Surely, I can't come again this quickly. It's an intense feeling. Wanting so desperately to come again, but not knowing if your body can handle it. Scary.

I pull away trying to get away from the overload of ecstasy, but he growls out and follows me. He lifts one of his own legs up so that his foot is planted on the bed—more traction.

"You're all fucking mine." He snarls and locks his hands around my legs.

"You're going to make me come again." I cry out and do my best to brace for the impact.

He's panting, grunting, and growling like a fucking beast as he pounds into me, just how I want it. Another orgasm rips its way through me, and I scratch my nails down his arms. I feel like I need to hit back, let him feel how intense this is. He shudders at the pain and grips onto me tighter. "Celine, fuck Celine, I'm coming. Deep. I'm so deep." His head drops down onto my chest as he slams into me hard three distinct times. A warmth fills me up inside as I feel his cock jerk with his orgasm. He moans loud, a deep guttural sound that tells me he is completely broken. He holds me close as he tries to catch his breath.

"Next time …" He gasps, "It'll be better next time."

"Oh hell, you planning to make me come to death." I throw my hands over my head and try to roll away. He chuckles, rolls over and pulls me back so I'm close to him. I snuggle into his chest and just let his heartbeat lull me to sleep. I've never felt so safe and cherished in my life, even if I know it may all be over soon.

CHAPTER

JAMESON

I'm so comfortable in bed right now and it's mostly because I have Celine cuddled up next to me. The woman wore me the fuck out. For someone who's never had sex before, I think that I've found me an addict. I can't be more fucking happy about that shit.

She turns slightly and rubs her ass on my midsection, even in her dreams she is feeling me up. "Celine." I growl out as I feel my dick getting hard again. I don't have the strength to fuck her again. I'm so fucking hungry that I'm about to eat the damn wood off the walls.

"Hmmm? One more?" She whispers and tries to toss her hands over my neck.

"No, later. Goddamn it woman, I'm not just some piece of meat." I chuckle. When her eyes open and a soft smile appears on her lips, I know that I would be her piece of meat if she asked me. I don't have a problem with that at all.

"Fine." She presses a hand to her throat. "Can I have some water?"

"Sure Darlin'. I'll be right back." I slip out of bed and throw on a pair of sweats. This is just the excuse I need to get the hell out of bed and get myself something to eat.

I stretch and walk out of the room, making my way to the small bar area where I can see Pirate and Yang talking. Yang seems to be his cool self like always, but Pirate looks agitated.

"What's up?" I say from where I am in front of my room.

Both sets of eyes jerk in my direction and kernels of fear bloom behind them. Something is wrong.

135

"Nothing yet. I don't know anything yet." Pirate speaks up. It's not like him to hide anything so this is new for me.

"Pirate, it's fucking obvious that it's not nothing. So, someone needs to tell me what the fuck is going on." Pirate doesn't open his mouth, so I direct my attention to Yang. "You going to tell me what the fuck is up, or do I need to wake Archer and call church?" It was still late enough in the middle of the night that not many people would be awake.

"Nah, man. Look we just don't know anything right now. It could be a traffic jam for all we know." Yang said trying to calm the situation down.

I squint my eyes at Pirate, and look at the time, it was almost 5 in the morning. He shouldn't fucking be here right now. This is the time that he makes his pickup from the casino. Any extra cash that needed to be placed elsewhere this is when he would make the pick up.

"What the fuck could be a traffic jam? Some one better tell me what is going on and right the fuck now or we are going to have a goddamn problem." I bark at the both of them.

"Fine. Look I was tired and drunk. I didn't think it would be that big of a deal. Mark was always asking to do something for us any way. He thought that if he could show us that he was responsible, we wouldn't be so mad that he'd let Monica in."

"Who?" I yell at them.

"We let Mark do pick up, but he's stopped answering us about thirty minutes ago. He should have been here ten minutes ago. He wouldn't steal from us Jameson. He might be a fuck up, but there is no way that he would do that shit." Pirate explains quickly.

"Motherfucker." I can feel the tension headache begin to pound in my head already. "How much is the drop?"

"It was about 250 thousand."

Pirate was the fucking treasurer, that much money was never supposed to touch anyone else's hands, but his own. There is no reason for him to even think to send Mark.

"You lazy piece of shit! I should fuck you up for this shit!" I push him hard in the chest, but he doesn't respond. He knows what he did is fucked up. "You better fucking pray that nothing has gone down or this shit is on your head."

Pirate nods his head and looks down to the bar.

I turn and walk over to the room on the right. Archer may be up by now. It is early enough, but I know he likes mornings to be with his woman. He is not going to like the fact that I have to interrupt him.

I knock on his door and here a gruff groan.

"Yeah?" Archer replies right away. He was still asleep.

"Sorry bro, we need you out here for a second." I say through the door.

"Copy."

I can hear his feet hit the floor. He isn't going to be happy about this shit at all.

After a few seconds he opens the door, all he has on is a pair of shorts and a wife beater. His hair is disheveled and there is still sleep in his eyes. "What's going on?" He asks.

"Pirate needs to divulge some fucking information to you." I say and we both walk back over to where Pirate is. Before we can reach him though, Pirate starts screaming.

"Fuck! Fuck! Mother fuck! Fuck!" Pirate picks up his stool and tosses it with all he has against the wall. It shatters and he screams out again. "You fucking bastards!"

Yang rushes over to us, panic in his wide eyes.

"What is it?" Archer asks. The sleep is gone, he's all with us right now.

"They fucking took them."

No! Oh fuck no!

"What the fuck are you talking about?" I ask.

"They sent over the CCTV footage and we can see a white van pull off with Mark and a few other people. They had guns and were holding some of the workers' kids in there too. Mark didn't have a choice."

"What the fuck? What is he even doing there?" Archer looks at Pirate, who has yet to even look in our direction.

"You think this was a hold up?" I ask Yang trying to steer the conversation away from Pirate. We don't need to dwell on Pirate's massive fuck up right now.

"I don't know ... especially with everything that is going on this could be something else. I can't call it." Yang shrugs.

"Yeah, I know. Well, we need to get on with this shit now. Let's roll." Archer basically runs to the back to get his stuff together. I race over to my room.

When I open the door, I see Celine is still safely tucked away under the blankets. I sit down next to her and run my hands over her arms to wake her up.

"Hmm? You ready?" She reaches for me, but when I don't let her pull me down, she wakes up more. "What's the matter?"

"Look we don't know for sure that anything is going down, but we have a few people missing. I'm going to head out with the guys to try and track them down. I need you to promise me that you will not leave. If I have to worry about where you are, that is just going to fuck with my head. Can I trust you to stay put?"

"Jameson, I don't like this. Do you think it's René? I need to go!" She tries to get out of bed, but I press my hand on her shoulder and keep her laying down.

"Did you not just hear what I said? You want me to worry about them and you? You really want to fuck me up like that right now?" I lay it on thick.

She sighs and her shoulders fall down, "No, I know you need to focus, but I don't want anything bad to happen to anyone. Not over me." She looks off to the side and I have to pull her face back so that she is looking at me.

"We know what we signed up for. This isn't a knitting circle, some-times bad shit happens. I have to keep my head straight if I'm going to make sure that I give this search and rescue my all. Promise me you will stay put."

"I'll stay put Jameson. I promise."

I nod and hurry to throw some clothes on. I slip my kutte on, give her a swift kiss and make my way out.

Now that I know my woman is safe, I can ride out with a clear fucking conscious. It's time for business.

We figure out that a white van picked up a few of our workers that were coming off the overnight shift and their children. Archer had made it so there was a childcare option at the casino for all the parents that needed it. He didn't want any of them worrying about their children, because they had to work the afterhours shift. All in all, it was 3 kids, 5 adults and Mark. His bike was found still parked in the back of the casino.

There was very little fighting that we can see from the area, but we would know more when we got inside to see the entire footage.

Gold Wings is one of the newest, yet most lucrative casinos in the area. Archer had bought the location from a scam artist who was on his last legs. The place was going to go under if no one took it over. We basically had to redo the place from the bottom up. Now you would never know that this place was a pig pen a few years back.

"I promise you, we have no idea what is going on." Herb, our floor manager says the minute we all walk into the back room. It's obvious that they have been going out of there mind with worry, but we already know that it's not someone in here that set this up.

"Show me what you got." Pirate snaps at him.

Herb turns the monitor in Pirate's direction and plays the in house security tape. We see the workers willingly get into the van. "Why would they do that? Why did they all just get in?" I ask Herb.

"We just recently started using dollar vans. You pay a dollar, and they will take you to the nearest bus stop. It's like a half a mile walk, which was hard for some of the folks to do. Especially with their little ones sleeping. They must have thought it was one of ours."

Pirate fast forwards the tape a few seconds to where we see Mark walking out of the casino, the bag I'm assuming with the cash secured across his body. As he walks toward his bike the sliding door to the van pops open and someone leans out with a gun in hand. There is something else in his other arm, but the angle doesn't allow us to see what it is. The small arm flailing back and forth makes me think it's one of the kids though. They must have threatened to kill one of them.

When Mark reaches for his weapon another gun is pointed out of the van and he slowly starts to walk toward them. The camera doesn't pick up sound, but I can see his face snarled up and his mouth going a million miles a minute.

"Fuck, ok, we know the make and model. We have to find this fucking van." Archer runs a hand through his perfect hair and looks around at everyone that is there. "Herb, make sure no one else gets into any of these cabs. If people are going home have someone from security take them."

"That is going to leave us open. If something is going on, then don't you think we need all the security we can get here at the casino, what if they come back to steal more money?" Herb questions.

Archer slams his hand down on the table. "I don't give a fuck about the money; these people work for me. Their safety is the most important. Make sure you figure out exactly who was taken and if they have any family members that I need to get in contact with." Archer stares Herb down for a second before he turns to the rest of us. "Let's go."

"I don't think this was just some random hit." I say as we all get to our bikes.

"Me neither. Whoever they are knows that we are going to be looking for our people. This was staged." Yang says.

"This shouldn't have gone down. This shit shouldn't have ever gone down." Pirate angrily starts up his bike.

"Stow that shit! We don't have time for you to lose your shit Pirate. This isn't your fault." Archer glares at Pirate for a second. I can't even imagine how fucked up he must feel right now. He was supposed to pick up this drop. Sure, they still might have taken the workers, but they wouldn't have been able to get Mark if he wasn't here for Pirate.

"Your right, let's go." Pirate put his lid back on and we roll out.

Hours later and even though we all split up, we were no closer to finding out where our people were. No one is calling for a ransom and no one is claiming it was them. Nothing but silence. By the time we all make it back to the clubhouse, it's the silence that is driving all of us out of our fucking minds.

"Did we check the cameras on the ferry and shit, maybe they took them somewhere else? At the marina?" Pirate asks Shyne who was busy talking to Herb down at the casino to see if there were any updates. Though with a shake of the head he quickly sent Pirate back into a rage. The longer we stayed without finding them, the worse Pirate got.

"Hey, what the fuck did I say? Do I need to pull you the fuck off this Pete?" Archer barks at Pirate.

"What? No. I need to help." Pirate replies his eyes wide as if he thinks that Archer really is pulling him off. I hope he doesn't, that would just drive Pirate further off the deep end.

"Then get your shit together. I need you to collect your head right now. I don't need no emotional fucks behind me if shit is about to go down."

"We got movement out here." Clay says from his position at the door. He has been on watch since this morning.

"Who is it?" I call out as I quickly make my way over there. Everyone else in the room does the same.

"I don't know, but I see a white van." He says and the tension in the room skyrockets. Why the fuck would they show up at our front door? This shit makes no sense.

"Fuck, that. Let's go get them." Pirate starts for the door, but Yang and Shyne hold him back. They are all thinking the same shit that I am, this shit is off.

"Are they alone?" I ask.

"No, there is another car behind it. Someone is getting out." Clay says from the door.

"Is it René?"

My head whips around to see Celine standing at the corner her eyes red from tears and her arms wrapped around her body.

"You don't need to be here right now." I growl at her, but don't make a move to go to her. I don't have time to fight with her.

"No, I don't know this one. He's younger. They're coming." Clay moves away from the door and he puts his hand behind him to get the gun that he has stashed at the small of his back.

There is a hard knock at the door. Clay looks to Archer who gives him the ok to open the door. It takes a second, but a young man walks in accompanied by two large guards.

"I think you have something that belongs to me." He says before he even figures out who he needs to be addressing. Either he wasn't used to intimidating a group or he just didn't care to try.

"Oh no." A loud gasp comes from Celine and from my peripheral vision I see her slide down the wall to the floor. It was our worst nightmare. René is responsible for this.

"Who?" I bark in her direction.

"Thomas, René's son." She cries out softly.

"Yes, that's right. I'm René's son and that woman over there is mine."

"Like fuck she is." I step forward once before Archer puts a hand out to stop me. The man is baiting me, but I'm not against taking it. I'll rip his fucking face off if he tries to take Celine.

"Look, I don't know what kind of deal you and your father think they worked out, but Celine wants no part of it." Archer is the one to speak up this time.

"That's a shame. I don't take kindly to someone not being able to pay their bets. And my father doesn't either. Her dad placed a bet and he lost. She is my payment."

"We can give you money if that is what you want, but we aren't giving you Celine." Yang says.

"Now what the fuck do I want with money. You're pretty, but you're not too bright." Thomas smirks. "Look I'm a busy man and want my property. Until I get it your people are going to keep dropping off."

"What the fuck is that supposed to mean? What is to stop us from putting a bullet in your fucking head right now?" Pirate asks.

"Well, your people in that van outside for one. I was under the impression that you would want them back alive. I can change that though. This time you won't be able to disarm the bomb in time." Thomas pulls out a small remote looking device and flips something up on it.

"No wait!" Archer puts his hands out.

"So what were you saying about putting a bullet in my head?" Thomas asks.

When no one responds he continues. "Celine love, you are really making this much harder than it should be. I thought we were at least friends, you going through all this trouble to stay away from me is really hurting my feelings. I don't appreciate it. I'm going to ask you once, are you going to come with me and end all this pain?" Thomas leans over so that he could speak directly to Celine, just the fact that he was doing that had me on edge.

"I don't want to be with you, Thomas. Moreover, you don't want to be with me either. You don't even like ..."

Before she could finish the statement, Thomas was screaming in anger, "Shut the fuck up you dumb gash. You don't know shit about me or what I like. I was going to treat you nice when I finally got my fucking hands on you, but now I'm going to take my fucking time showing you everything I like. By the time me and all my friends are finished, you'll be split open from ass to pussy begging me to kill you. Then just to get you the fuck out of my face, I'll tie your father's dead body to your feet and throw you in the fucking Mississippi river. Don't you ever tell me what the fuck I want." He growls.

"Fuck you Thomas, I'll throw myself off a fucking bridge before I become anything for you." Celine was crying, but still she continues to fight back. The tears were just from emotional overload.

"Fine have it your way. I have shit to handle. If any of you try to stop me or harm me on my way out, I will blow the fucking van up. Have you ever had to identify a friend from just using random body parts? It's like a huge jigsaw puzzle, quite mentally stimulating." Thomas pulls on his sleeves and shoots Celine a wink that has me growl in contempt. I will rip his fucking eyeballs out of his face.

"No one is going to fuck with you." Archer says.

Everyone stares at him for a second, but I know he's right. We have to get our people back safe and sound. If that means we have to let Thomas walk out of here with a looming threat over our heads than that is what we are going to do.

"Good, nice to know there is at least one smart bastard here. I'll give you all some time to think about how much little Celine here is worth to you. I'll be back to collect what is mine when you make the right decision." He turns and just as suddenly as he arrived, leaves.

We wait until we hear Thomas' car start and pull away before we all rush out of the clubhouse. All of us try to get to Mark and the rest of the hostages.

"Mark!" Pirate calls out, he burst through us all and races the few hundred feet out to where the van is.

I can see movement and hear dull screams, but there is no one coming out. Maybe there are still some of Thomas and René's men in there with them. "Pirate hold up! We don't know who is in the van." I call out to him trying to get him to take a breath and assess the situation.

"Fuck that, I have to get him out!" He yells back and we all follow him. If one brother goes in, we are all going in. Pirate makes it to the van and looks into the small round window in the back. "It's them. It's them." Pirate calls out as we all make it to where he is.

"Let's get them out." Shyne calls out as he goes to the side where the sliding door is.

"Wait!" Clay yells out, but he's too late.

A small white hot explosion causes me to squint and in that one second I can see my life flash before my eyes. At least I think that is what I see, I can't focus long enough to know what the fuck I saw.

We all fall to the ground as a wave of fire begins rolling out from the bottom of the van and licking up the sides of the vehicle.

"Oh fuck! Oh no, no!" Archer jumps up from the ground and tries open the doors.

"Please! Help!" Screams barely audible over the roar of fire that appeared to suck up all the sound in the area assaulted my ears.

"Fuck! Mark! Open the door!" Pirate grabs onto the side of the door, but no matter how much he pulls it doesn't open.

"It's fucking welded shut!" I yell, rushing to the passenger side door to maybe get them out that way. The bastards had welded all the fucking doors shut. The driver side door was dented in too, so that it couldn't be opened that way.

"Fuck!" Shyne howls as he sticks his arm into the flames that were steadily engulfing more and more of the van.

"Ahhh! No! Momma! Momma!" A little kid screams inside.

"Goddamn it! It won't fucking open!" Mark screams out from inside the van, coughing between each word. "Shit! Get us the fuck out!" The panic lacing his words and the van violently shaking back and forth as the fire continues to burn and sizzle all around us.

"Go get a fucking crowbar! Fire extinguisher, fucking anything!" Archer bellows out as he continues to try and find a way to get to the people in the van. He pulls his gun and tries to shoot the lock, but it just dents the side.

Yang runs back with a crowbar, but even with Pirate, myself, and Shyne on it we don't get the door to budge. Not only is it welded shut, but the heat from the flames is now warping the metal. It's too hot for us to stay on it for long.

Shyne tries to get to the front of the van and break the window only to find out that there is a grate in place. There are grates on every window. They didn't want us to get them out of there. That bastard Thomas knew we wouldn't be able to. The small circle window at the back of the van blows out and the screams that leak out make me feel like I'm in the deepest level of hell. They bang on the hot metal as it rocks back and forth with their efforts to escape. Coughing and crying. The crying. So much crying. The sound rises to an impossible pitch as the innocent people inside are burned alive. Sweat rolls down my face as the intense heat continues to rise and I have no choice, but to fall back away from the fire. The strong stench of burning meat assaulting my nose with each breath.

Shyne turns and vomits all over the ground as the cries of pain and death surround us.

"Ma! Mommy! Ahhh!" A child screams out and I swear I can hear a woman saying they love them. Trying her hardest to soothe her baby in their final moments.

"Help! Please!"

"Save us! Oh God please save us!"

"Fuck! Fuck! Help! Please help me!" Mark cries out from inside the burning van. His voice croaking from the smoke and the pain.

The screams are becoming quieter, but Pirate is still trying to find a way in as the rest of us realize that no matter what we do now everyone in that van is dead.

"Hold on! I'm not going to fucking leave you! We're here!" Pirate rushes toward the van again, but it's so hot he has to take a step back. "Fuck! Mark!" He screams and then tries again. This time he makes it to the side of the door and tries again futilely to open the sliding door.

Half of his body is deep in the flames, but his brother is in that van. He is going to do whatever he can to try and get him out. When his pants and kutte catch fire, I grab hold of him and pull him back. Tackling him to the ground, I use my hands to snuff out the flames.

Everyone is sitting around, the screams have stopped and the flames on the van are still raging. Now they are coming from inside, small tufts of flames rolling out the small window.

"No, we have to help them! Please!" Pirate yells out and tries again to get to the van.

"It's over man. I'm sorry. It's over." I hold my brother as he roars in pain. There is nothing that we can do for any of them now.

CHAPTER 23

JAMESON

The fire burned the van until we were able to use the few extinguishers that we had to douse the flames. Even with three extinguishers it took us over an hour to get everything under control. When I walk back into the clubhouse, I can see everyone that is still around. The old ladies and some of the club bunnies are huddled together crying. Daria rushes over to Archer when he comes in bringing him into an embrace. Celine sees me and tries to do the same, but I push her away. I can't handle all the hands and emotions right now.

I walk into my room and just sit on the bed. It's been a long time since I've lost a brother and despite knowing that this isn't the same thing as what I went through in the field, it still feels raw.

"You blame me … don't you?" Celine says from where she is standing at my door.

I clench my fist and bite the inside of my mouth, so I don't flip out on her. I don't have time for this shit. I just heard a bunch of people being burned to death. My skin is singed and my fucking lungs hurt. I don't have the strength to go a few rounds with her.

"Celine, I don't know what you are talking about right now, but just leave it alone."

"No, I'm not going to leave it alone. What is going to have to happen before you realize this isn't worth it!" She storms in my direction and stops directly in front of me.

I can't hold back anymore. I don't have the restraint to hold back anymore. "What the fuck is your problem Celine! Do you think I need this shit right now! For fuck's sake people are fucking dead and you are over here making it about you! This shit isn't about you. Fuck!" I stand up and push by her so I can get out the door.

"It is though. Can't you see that? He's not going to stop. None of them are going to stop. This is going to keep on happening."

"So what are you suggesting that we just give up, because that is not how this shit works."

"It needs to Jameson." She stands up and grabs my face. "I can't just sit here hiding behind your steel walls waiting for him to take out your entire family. You have to let me go."

"No. I'm not going to let some little fuck intimidate me into giving up what is mine. And even if you weren't, its people like us that have to stand up to people like him and his father. What the fuck kind of world would we be living in, if no one puts bastards like René in his fucking place."

"I don't think it's the right time to teach him that lesson."

"No right now is the perfect fucking time. I'm not going to tell you this again. I don't blame you for what is going on. You are not the first person that René has tried to fuck over, but we have to make sure you are the last one. He needs to know that no matter what he does in this town we are going to be here to fuck him up if he gets out of line. I don't blame you, fuck I don't think anyone here fucking blames you. You are just caught in a fucked up situation, one we are not going to let you handle on your own."

Tears bloom in her eyes and she lays her head on my chest, "I'm so sorry, Jameson. I'm so sorry." She wraps her arms around me and this time I let her. I don't think this is more about me, but more about her. I don't blame her, but she surely must blame herself.

"I know Darlin', we are going to get through this."

She sniffles and nods her head.

I kiss the top of her head and wait for her to calm down. I'm not going to let her go and there is nothing that anyone says that is going to force me to do it.

"Did you hear anything from Herb?" I ask Archer from my seat at the table. Once we were all able to compose ourselves and properly take care of the bodies in our back yard, Archer calls church.

"No, there hasn't been anyone coming or going that we need to be concerned about. He says it's business as usual."

Pirate sits in his seat, but I can tell that he isn't really here. He's not going to be alright for a long time.

"Fuck ... oh fuck ..." Shyne says and I watch as his eyes squint closed. The phone in his hands cracking and moaning from the increased pressure of his hands.

"What?" Archer asks him.

I take a breath, knowing that whatever Shyne is looking at on his phone isn't going to be good. We can't afford to get any more bad news. Not right now.

"They sent us a message via social media. Our account has been flagged, but someone sent me a copy of the video."

"What the fuck! What do you mean social media? Like fucking Facebook? You have got to be shitting me!" I pull my phone out and try to remember the fucking password to the club's page. We only put one up, because Daria thought it was a good idea for people to know the guys behind the casino and the shooting range. I rarely fucking checked it. In fact, I don't think anyone besides Daria actually checks it.

Archer growls in frustration as he jumps out of his seat, slamming his chair back against the wall. "Fuck! What the fuck is this?"

Shyne sends everyone the video via email. "I don't know what it is, but the caption said, you take mine, I'll take yours."

When I open the video, I hear a woman with a bag over her head screaming, but only for a second. Someone off camera shoves her head down into a clear tote full of water. The woman fights and tries to get up, but the man doesn't stop. It's not long before the woman stops fighting altogether and her hands fall to the side. The video is all of three minutes long, no words are spoken. Nothing is heard, besides the woman drowning and fighting for her life, but I had to watch it again.

"What the hell did the message say? No one says anything in this video." Archer says and looks back over to Shyne. "Are they just trying to flag the authorities or some shit? I don't understand why they would do that shit."

"The caption only said that we took theirs, so they took ours." Shyne responds.

"Fuck, I'll make sure Daria looks into it. I don't want whoever it was to be able to post again-" Archer stops talking and turns to me. I'm tapping my feet hard as I replay the video again.

"No, please no." I mutter to myself and pull the phone as close as I can to my face.

"Jameson?" Archer questions me, but I can't respond my attention is completely transfixed on the woman in the video.

"Fuck no ..." My throat closes up and I feel the burn in my eyes as tears threaten to spill.

"Jameson, what the fuck is the matter?" Yang barks at me and his cool demeanor is gone.

"That's her fucking ring. That's her ring." I reply, it's the only thing that I can say. The ring, it's the only thing that I can focus on.

"What?" Shyne asks and opens the video again. Besides the horrendous video of the woman being drowned there is nothing in the background, her hand is the only thing visible. It looks like they did that on purpose.

"That's Monica's fucking ring!" I roar. Dread creeps up into my chest as I replay it again. I'm trying to find anything that would let me know that it was just a fucking replica or one that just looked like hers. It wasn't though, I would know that fucking ring anywhere. It was custom made and she never took it off. Back when we first got together Monica had a thing for butterflies. I had proposed to her, giving her a custom engagement ring with a butterfly on it. The wings were light blue and light green gems while there was a single teardrop shaped solitaire diamond directly in the middle. I didn't have much back then, but I'd made sure to get her a ring that I knew she would love and she did.

"What, no ... Are you fucking sure?" Archer asks and I can see him pulling up the video on his phone again.

"When was the last time that you spoke with her?"

"The other day when she made that whole scene here. She told me that she was going to go up to Maine and start fresh. I told her that we weren't ever getting back together. I gave her some money and then she was on her way." I replay the video again, searching desperately for anything that would prove that it wasn't her. I couldn't find a thing yet.

"Goddamn it!" Archer put his head back, "Ok. Let's make sure first."

"Call her." Pirate says from where he is sitting.

That hadn't even occurred to me, but that could be an easy way to find out for certain. If she picked up, I would know for sure that it wasn't her.

I fumble with my phone, but my hand is shaking so much that I can't get the fucking video off.

"I got it." Yang says and he pushes his phone into the center of the table. He reaches over to slide it open and calls Monica's phone. It wasn't surprising that he had her number. They all had her number, just in case something happens to me or they needed to find me. She would have been one of the main contacts that they would have gone through to get me. At one time she was the most important person in my life.

The phone rings two times before someone picked up.

"Monica!"

"No, try again." A man's voice replies.

My entire body crumbles, it was her on the video.

"Where the fuck is Monica?" Archer is the one to continue the conversation.

"Monica is dead, but you obviously know that already. Give me what belongs to me. Give Celine back to me or I promise you that this is just the tip of the fucking iceberg. Oh, I think you'd like to know. Your boy, I think his name was Mark, he never gave you up. He was a good kid. Sucks you chose to sacrifice him." The line goes dead before anyone can say anything else.

"Motherfucker! Fuckers!" Pirate yells and picks up Yang's phone tossing it into the side wall.

"Oh fuck ... Monica ..." I press play again, watching my ex-wife struggle for her life. My vision blurs as the tears roll down my face. Yes, she did me wrong, but had still been my wife. I loved her before and had dreams of her having my children at one point. Once upon a time, she had been my everything.

"Stop, bro. Stop watching that shit." Bones tries to take the phone away from me, but I have it clenched tight like a gold bar in my hand. This is all that's left of her.

"Jameson, stop. Don't torture yourself like this. There was nothing you could've done." Archer says from where he is.

Wasn't there? She came here. She came here, because we knew that there was a chance of family being targeted. She came here and I'd sent her away like she was an unwanted dog. Threw some money at her and just let her ride the hell out of my world straight into the arms of the bastards that would take her life.

The words Celine spoke to me earlier echo in my head. My family was being picked apart, because I refused to let them take her. Was she really worth this?

CHAPTER

24

CELINE

The clubhouse is in fucking shambles and everywhere I turn I can see them giving me the side eye. Jameson swears to me that no one here thinks that this is my fault, but that doesn't mean he is telling me the truth. He could just be telling me what I want to hear to make sure that I don't leave. I don't know how long I will be able to just sit back and let everyone that he knows end up dead. He told me about what they'd done to Monica. The woman was crazy, but that didn't mean that I wanted her dead.

I walk out of the room and sit down in the small kitchen that hadn't had a meal cooked in it for the past three days. I didn't know these people very well. Still, I hate that I had anything to do with the fact that they were hurting so bad. I hate that they had to sacrifice so much for me to be safe.

I see Daria at the table with her laptop and a specialized modem attached to it. I didn't want to bother her, but out of everyone here she seemed to be the only one who still liked me. At least she didn't look as if she wanted my head to pop off at the closest possible opportunity.

"You busy?" I ask even though I can see her staring hard at the screen in front of her. I just want someone to talk to. Jameson is around, but he hasn't been sleeping well. Even though he is trying to keep a brave face for me, I can tell that he is upset about what went down with his ex-wife. That night he told me that he'd cried for her. I had to hold him while he mourned for the woman who's place I'd taken. It was hard, but it was something that I had to do.

"Nah, not really. I'm not getting any further than I've already been." She shrugs her shoulders and pats the table signaling that she wants me to sit down.

I take a second to look at what she is doing and it's not something that I'm used to seeing. It's a whole bunch of computer code, Html I think and maybe some other things. I have no idea what any of it means though. Daria is a kick ass techy. From what Jameson told me about her, she is their go to when they are needing any type of information that they can't figure out from normal sources.

"What are you looking for?'

"The owner of the account that posted the video to our page. I'm not coming up with anything new though. All I know is that it was posted from an I.P. address that says it is located in the state."

"You can get the location of people just from what they post on Facebook?" I ask completely bewildered. That seemed like a complete breach of privacy to me, probably something that could come in handy though.

"You would be surprised at how much information people put on the web without actually realizing it. Everything on the internet leaves a trail. Most people think that once you delete or log out of a site that all evidence of it vanishes. Not the case, it's all there just waiting for someone like me to dig up the information. Yeah, usually I would be able to find out, but these guys made sure to block their location. They were careful and made sure that whatever I.P. they were using was also bouncing from other regions. It's almost impossible for me to track them down without them posting another video. I don't think they are stupid enough to do that." She looks away from the computer and focuses her attention on me, "What about you? What's going on?"

"Oh nothing much ... you know just responsible for a whole slew of deaths. A typical day." I half joke then drop my head in my hands. I want to just break down. I'd always been taught to get back up no matter how hard you are pushed down, but how do I beat this? How do I beat a crazy mad man like René? Right now, I'm not seeing a way to do it.

"Do you seriously believe that shit?" Daria asks me.

When I turn my gaze to her, I can see that she is glaring at me and not just with annoyance, but with clear anger.

"How could I not believe that?"

"Celine, I know that there is a lot of shit going on right now and things are hard. But my brothers and my husband have sacrificed so much, not for you, but for their way of life and for the way of life that we all want. Don't cheapen what they've done by trying to shoulder all the blame. You aren't the fuck that doesn't know not to try and sell people. You are not the one that lit that van on fire. You are not the one who killed Monica. None of that was you … so don't try to force that on yourself. I don't want to hear anything like that ever again. Either you are going to be with us here helping to figure out how we get René and his crazy ass son out of business or you are going to bring us all down. Don't make Jameson fight for you by himself." Daria looks away. She takes a deep breath, trying to stem her anger.

"I'm sorry, I know you're right. I know it's not my fault, but I don't want anyone else to be brought into my drama. I just want you all to come away from this whole and alive. That's all."

"What about you? Do you not deserve to come out of this whole? Do you not deserve to be happy with Jameson? Why isn't that option on the table?"

I open my mouth to answer, but for the life of me I don't have one thing that I would be able to say to her. There is no response as to why I'm not allowed to live my life to the fullest and be happy. I wanted my father to be alive and safe, Jameson to be mine, and the club to be okay. But when was I going to start worrying about me being ok?

I shook off her question and switched to something I thought was more appropriate—her being a hacker. "How did you learn how to do all this?"

"Oh, this is nothing, you should see what Pooh over in Puerto Rico can do. I mean that man is a freaking magician. Maybe I should be reaching out to him about this. Honestly, I went to school for web design. The rest of it just came as I continued to tinker."

"That is crazy to be able to find someone even if they aren't located anywhere on the map. Looks like it is an invasion of privacy, but if it finds folks like René then I am all for it.

"Oh trust me, there is so much more that I can find than just where a person is located. In fact, if you were to see all of the web browser histories that I have gone through you would think twice about ever using the computer again." Daria laughs and she looks back to the computer. I want to help her, but I know that there is nothing that I can do. She is the wiz not me. The most that I can do is offer her some company. I think that will suit me just fine.

"Are you ever going to tell Jameson what is going on with you or are you going to keep on pretending that this isn't happening?" Daria switches back to the hard conversation, as she opens up another tab on her computer.

"I did tell him. I told him to let me go, but he acted like I was crazy. I mean there is nothing more I can say to him to prove that having me here is the worst thing that he can do right now."

"The worst thing? Really, I think having you here is the best thing that has happened to Jameson."

"I've caused him nothing but trouble."

"He's falling in love with you." Daria says plainly and my mouth snaps shut.

"What?" I ask when I'm finally able to get my mouth to open again.

"Please girl, you can't tell me that you don't see it. That man is falling so damn hard in love with you. There is nothing that could be happening that would make him give you up."

I chuckle slightly, but don't respond to her. If that is true than it just puts a whole new piece into the pie. He'll never let me go, even if it's the best thing for him. Jameson will sacrifice everything if it means that he gets to keep me. I'm happy if he feels this way, but I know that with all that is happening right now this can't be the way. I won't let him sacrifice himself for me. I can't live with that.

"You ok Darlin'." Jameson walks up behind me as I put the phone back down on the hook. I've been wandering around the clubhouse for most of the day. Keeping myself occupied for as long as I can before I move on to do something else. I had even scrubbed the bathrooms.

Not the highlight of my week. Every so often I would use the club's phone to try and call my father again. Still, I haven't heard anything from him. By now I was sure that he was dead and gone. I was just waiting for someone to reach out to me and let me know where I would be able to pick up the body. My father was tough as nails, but I just couldn't see him getting through something like this.

I hang the phone back up on the cradle and turn to Jameson, "Yeah, I was just checking to see if I had any messages from my father."

"Anything?"

"No, nothing." I search his eyes looking for the hatred that I know he feels for me, but I don't see anything. I see sadness and adoration, but no anger.

"You left me alone up there." He pulls me close to him.

"Yeah, well you were snoring like a lawn mower. It was either leave or go deaf." I smirk and he pulls me closer, planting a kiss on my lips.

"You promise, you're not fucking going anywhere?" He asks as he places his forehead against mine.

"I'm here with you, Jameson. You can trust me."

He backs up slightly and nods, then he drags his hands down his face. "I don't know why your father hasn't reached out to you. Some-how, I know that René hasn't killed him, I'm sure that would be one of the first things that he would have shown off."

I cringe at the thought of my father being the next target for torture. He's right though, René likes to show off what he's done. There is no way that he would have killed my father and not told me. In fact, I don't even think there is a chance that my father has been gone for so long without them figuring out where he is. My father was a big man, fast, and strong, but he never knew when he was beat. Dad would have come back by now and they must have gotten him. Maybe they were planning to use him as bait, but they wouldn't do that via phone. René and his son like strong visual impact. If they were going to use my father to draw me out, they would do it by either bringing him here or via video like they had done with Monica.

"I don't know either." I tell Jameson, letting the conversation drop. It's not because I don't want to talk to him, but my brain is already going a million miles per minute.

"Jameson, let me talk to you for a second." Bones calls out for him and Jameson walks off.

I take that as my cue. I rush over to where Daria had left her computer on the table in the kitchen. I don't know exactly what I'm looking for. Despite that, I have a bad feeling as I pull up my email that I'm about to find much more than what I want to find.

I close my eyes and cover my mouth before a cry can escape my mouth. Dozens upon dozens of emails are in there all from an address I don't know. Every single one of them have a video attachment on them. I look around the space to make sure that I'm alone and lower the volume on the computer. When I open up the attachment, I see a part of my worst nightmare. Daddy is tied up in a basement of sorts and they are beating him with bats.

The next attachment is more of the same, only this time they are beating him with crow bars. Every one of the emails has the same message.

One of yours for the return of what's mine.

They had only sent these to me thinking that I would see them and run to wherever they are.

They were right.

I pull up the latest email and wipe away the tears that have fallen from my eyes. This one came in this morning. I hit reply and ask where I should meet them.

The response hits my email seconds later.

There is an address and directions to come alone. If I do, they will let my father live. If I don't, they will kill us both on the spot and then continue to take our debt out on the Wings of Diablo. How do I do this?

The club will follow me if I tell them, not just Jameson, but all of them. If I don't tell them they will think that René managed to get a hold of me and they will still come looking for me.

There are no other options here. I have to do this, but maybe I don't have to do it completely on my own.

I close out of my email and open up a few other websites, some of them are questionable. I make my way upstairs and pen a letter to Jameson. I'd made a promise to him that I wouldn't leave him, but I have to do this. I leave the letter under his pillow, someplace that isn't very visible.

I need to give myself some time, enough that I can get my father out of there and to safety.

I go into the bathroom and open the small window, but not before disabling the alarm. They will figure out sooner or later that I've disabled it, but I'm praying its later. I slither my way through the small space and take off running before my feet even touch the ground.

Jameson will be disappointed and scared. However, I'm praying his brothers will keep him calm long enough for him to figure out that I'm not leaving. I'm just showing him the way.

CHAPTER 25

CELINE

The door to the small nightclub opens the second I step up to it. I don't see a peep hole or a camera, but there must be one.

The second I walk in a bright light blinds me and I have to put my hand up to my face to shield my eyes.

"MMM … Mm!" I hear someone moaning, but my eyes can't focus on my surroundings.

"It took you long enough to come." René's voice echoes in the open space.

Finally, my eyes adjust to the light around me. I can see that the nightclub I am standing in has been gutted, there is nothing in the place besides a few boxes, a couple chairs and three tables, and what used to be a bar. No one would ever think to look at this place.

"Mmm!"

My head turns towards the sound of the person moaning. It's my dad. My eyes water as I see the state that he is in. They have him attached to a table, literally. His hands are pinned down with long nails into one of the tables so that he can't lift them. It's a gruesome sight and one that lets me know that my father's boxing days are over. I want to run to him, but I don't want to heighten my emotions any more than they are. "I'm here now. Let him go." I say looking around for Thomas or René.

The both of them walk out of the shadows like two mafia bosses in a straight to DVD, B rated movie. I want to roll my eyes at their dramatics.

"No, I think you might need to be punished a bit further. You've wasted quite a bit of our assets trying to run all around town. What do you think son? Maybe we need to teach her a lesson?" René turns to Thomas who is just staring at me.

"Yeah, let me get my pliers." He replies as a sly smile works its way up his face.

"Pliers, no … I bought her for you so you can continue our line. How are pliers going to help you do that?"

"Continue the line? Like babies?" Thomas asks.

"Of course, your brothers have already given me choices, but you are the only one that is holding back. Why do you think I've gone through all this trouble to bring her back to you? I could have had her killed days ago for her disrespect alone. But you made it quite clear that if there were to be anyone to bear your children it would be her."

"Well yeah, I mean …" Thomas begins to stutter and I know that he is worried that his father is about to figure out his little secret. "I'll make sure that I don't mess up anything down there. I can just take a few teeth out or something."

"No!" René roars out and glares at his son. "Just like I don't fucking appreciate her wasting my fucking time, I don't appreciate you wasting it either. Son or no son, if you sent me on a wild fucking goose chase to locate this woman and you are not intending to use her in the way she should be used … We are going to have a goddamn problem. You want to punish her, fine, she needs to be punished. I have the perfect way for you to do that." René grabs his son by the collar and quite forcefully pulls him in my direction. "Show her father exactly what he signed her up for."

What? My eyes widen in shock. He can't possibly be saying what I think he is saying.

"MMMM, mm, mmph, MMM!" My father screams something inaudible. Although from the way he is shaking his head and kicking his legs around I know he is threatening them.

"Fine, if that's what you think is best dad. I'll do it."

"Emmett, Cyril, grab her!" I hear footsteps from the side of me. Two guards that I didn't realize were there, try to grab me.

I take a step back and before I realize what is going on my hands are snapping out perfect combinations.

Jab, jab, cross. One of them drops to the ground as the one behind me grabs me around my arms. I swing my head back and make perfect contact with his nose. He lets me go just as the first guard gets back up and rushes me. His head is down, the absolute worse position for him to be in. I pull my hand back and come upwards in a perfectly placed uppercut. The resounding click of his teeth is satisfying as he falls down to the ground unconscious.

The man behind me tries to grab me again, but I fall back into my stance and swing another hook to his face. Apparently, no one had taught these bastards how to keep their fucking hands up when they fight.

"Enough!" René screams out. I look up to see he has a gun pressed to my father's head.

"No ... Daddy!" I cry and the guard I was just beating up grabs me around my arms. I try to swing my head back, but he must have caught on from the last time since he moves out of the way. He drops me on the other side of the table in front of my father.

"Mmm. Mmm ... mmm ..." My father is starting to hyperventilate as I fight against the man that is holding me down.

Thomas makes his way over to me and starts to peel his shirt off. I was wrong before, he is sickly skinny. The sight of his thin, bird like chest makes me want to vomit. I think I could easily kick my foot through his chest he is that damn skinny.

There is no way that he would have the strength to hold me down by himself, he is going to need his guard here for the whole thing.

"Stop, wait! Just stop!"

"No, you should have just come to me like you were supposed to. Now this has to be so much worse than what it should be."

My eyes dart over to my father and I can see that he is going to lose his shit. His face is beet red and he is trying to pull his impaled hands free from the nails holding him in place. This can't be happening. It's one thing for this to happen to me behind closed doors, but this will kill him. Dad will die knowing that he let something like this happen to me and all he could do was sit right there next to me watching.

"Don't fuck around with it Thomas, fuck that bitch!" René screamed and his son flinched.

I kick out, but I don't connect with anything besides the table that I was laying on.

"Fuck I can't wait for this bitch to be brought down a few pegs." The guard who is holding my arms says.

"MMM, MMMph ... Mmm!"

I can't hear what my father is screaming. I wish I could at least talk to him right now, reassure him that I'll be okay.

Thomas pulls my legs out straight and crawls onto the table over me. He grabs my hair hard enough for tears to spring to my eyes. "You stupid bitch! I knew you weren't worth my time. If you would have just fucking agreed to give me what the fuck I wanted, we wouldn't be in this fucking situation, now would we? This is all your fucking fault, no use in crying now." Thomas bends down and licks the side of my face.

"Please, don't do this." I whisper out. Only that doesn't do anything, but enrage him further. He pulls a knife from his waistband and begins to cut the fabric from my skin. Every once in a while the tip of the blade nicks my skin and causes me to flinch in pain.

"I'm going to fuck you until you beg me to stop!" He growls out as he continues to take his time torturing me and threatening what is to come. He reaches down and undoes his pants only pulling them down slightly but enough for me to feel skin.

He presses himself down on me. I expect to feel his hard little dick digging into my skin, but I feel nothing, only squishy flesh. He's not hard, not even a little bit. How the fuck can he rape me if he can't get it up? I look over to my father for a second, hoping that he knows I'm just doing whatever I think I need to do in order to survive this still intact. I don't know if this is going to work, but I will give it my best shot.

I change my tactic, "I've been looking forward to this." I whisper and look deep into Thomas' eyes.

He stutters, "What?"

"I'd thought my running away was because I didn't want you. But if I'm honest, I do want you. I was just scared of your business ... I mean this is all a bit much. But I'm so excited for you right now. Fuck me, I can't wait to feel you deep inside of me Thomas."

His face literally turns green. I shy to the side, because I think he is going to throw up.

"You don't mean that shit." Thomas says as he leans up away from me.

"Oh yes I do, I mean every word of it." I lift one of my legs and wrap it around his pulling him closer to me.

René laughs out from where he is, "I knew it. This one is a freak. Come on son, show her what she is getting herself into. She'll be begging for your cock by the time you finish! Show her!" René pushes his son forward.

"I thought ... I thought this was about punishment." Thomas says out loud, trying to move away from me.

"Punish me. I'm so wet waiting for you to punish me. I'll take all of your cock for my punishment." I say in my most vulgar tone. I chance looking in my father's direction and he is no longer moaning, but the look in his eyes displays pure disgust. It's not every day that you get to hear your recently deflowered virgin daughter talk about how much they want someone's cock. He must be beating my ass in his mind.

"No, you're not going to force me to give you my rod for your own pleasure." Thomas pushes further off of me. He's more than ready to get off the table and leave me intact. I had found his button. He didn't like women. I don't know if there was anything that I could do besides raping him myself that would have gotten him to do what his father asked of him. If he just wanted to hurt me that was one thing, he would have used something to molest me with. However, if he thought that he was actually going to have to have sex with me he couldn't do it.

"Force you? I'm not forcing you, baby, I belong to you remember. Bought and paid for ... Claim me, fuck me until I cry for you to stop. That is what this is all about isn't it?" I pout, the silly look on my face makes me want to roll my own eyes.

"Why the fuck is your dick not in her pussy right now?" René asks, the laughter on his face just moments ago gone. "I got her for your birthday present. Every other woman that I've brought you, you've complained that there is something wrong with them. But now I bring the woman you claim is perfect for you, yet you still refuse to fuck her." He seems in shock.

"I can't dad, I don't want to do this here. Maybe when I get her back home and there aren't so many people watching. How the fuck can you expect me to do anything when there are so many damn people in the fucking room." Thomas tries to force a little anger in his tone, like his father shouldn't have even asked him to embarrass himself like that.

"No, fuck that. You will fuck her right now in front of me. You will plant your seed in this girl right the fuck now. I need men not fucking sissies." René snarls out and Thomas' jaw drops. He knew. He knew that his son was gay, and this was his way to prove that he wasn't.

"Dad, I'm not a sissy."

"Oh? I hear the rumors, boy. I hear that you spend your nights in those clubs. I can't have that shit associated with my name. Son or not, if you don't prove to me right now that you love cunt, you are going to be the next one nailed to a fucking table."

"What the fuck dad, I'm not a fucking sissy!" Thomas yells at his father and takes a step away from me. The guard is still holding my arms down and the last thing that I want to do is to anger any of them more. I stay completely still and let this play out the way that it will.

My father squints at me clearly trying to figure out what the fuck I'm doing, but he doesn't say anything. I give him a wink to let him know that I'm ok and he shakes his head in disbelief.

"You say that, but why the fuck is she not speared on your fucking dick right now, if you're not? I will not have any wussies in my family. You want any part of what I've built, you show me right the fuck now that you know what the fuck you are doing."

Thomas stares at him for a second his mouth opening and closing like a fucking fish before he turns to me and licks his dry lips. "Fine, you want me to fuck this dirty bitch I will. I never want to hear about this shit again."

"Never again son. Never again. Make me proud."

Thomas pulls his pants down further and I can see his flaccid member lying flat against his ball sack. He didn't even have a fucking semi right now. Nothing about this was turning him on. "Take her fucking pants off." He orders and the guard roughly rips the rest of the fabric, not that there was much left to cover my modesty.

"Get the hell off of me!" I curse out as the guard tears my panties off as well. There was no fucking getting out of this shit now.

"Fuck that. Hold still." Thomas says as he begins to stroke his own dick, his eyes closed probably thinking about someone else. Ever so slowly he began to get hard. "Don't even think about cumming on my cock or I'll slit your pretty throat right the fuck here." Thomas snaps at me as he walks back over to the table that my father is still nailed down to and where I'm lying completely naked.

He kneels between my legs and continues to pump his dick, painfully hard with his hand. Instead of getting more erect it seems as if he is losing his hard on.

"Fuck it." he leans down and even though he is only semi hard works to force his way inside of me. He forces my pussy lips open wide with his hands. Stretching them far enough that I scream out in pain. He groans at that, getting off on my pain.

I shut my mouth and try not to cry again. I won't give him the satisfaction. I turn my head back to my father. He is crying and moaning through the gag.

"Shhh, it's alright. Close your eyes dad. Just close your eyes." I soothe in his direction trying to get him to not be here with me right now. If this is how this was going to go down, I didn't need him to remember it. I didn't want him to see me like this. "Please dad. Don't watch."

He exhales hard and closes his eyes.

I do the same.

I had only one more place to hide, in my own mind. Thomas or René couldn't get me there. I would just go away until this was over.

CHAPTER

26

JAMESON

After I sat with Bones for a little while making sure that we had everything we needed to properly bury anymore of our people I went to sit at the bar. My mind is swimming with all the bullshit that is going on. Celine is the only damn peace I have right now. For someone I've known for less than a fucking month her hold on me is deep and unmovable.

We've all been pretty much wandering around here without much to do. The joys of being on lockdown. René was still popping up all around town, but no one wanted to go against him. We were all scared that he was going to get someone in our families and hurt them. Something he had already proved he can do.

"What the fuck!" Yang says loudly as I pick up the brew from the bar and press it to my lips. Yang's exclamation jerks me out of my numb state. What the hell was going on now?

"What is it? What?" I ask hopping off the chair.

"Yang, you get a message?" Archer says from across the room. He and Daria are standing by the side door.

"Shit!" Yang got up from his seat and ran like the devil himself was after him. The one word none of us wanted to hear tossed back over his shoulder as he made his way to the rooms on the right. "Breach!"

"Fucking hell!" I take off close behind him, the footsteps of my patchmate on my tail. They got in. Someone broke into the clubhouse. How the fuck is that even possible and why didn't the fucking alarms go off?" When Yang stops in front of my room and bursts in, my fucking heart drops to my feet. No. No. Fuck no.

"Celine!" I scream for her, but I don't get an answer.

When I push myself into the room, Yang is in the bathroom and Celine is nowhere to be found.

"Where the fuck is Celine?" Pirate asks once he gets inside my room and can see that she's not here.

I can't stop my brain from feeling like it's going to drop out of my ears. This shit can't be happening again, I can't be losing her too. What the fuck!

"Hold up, just hold up. Check the rest of the compound she could still be here." Archer barks out his command. The rest of my brothers make moves to search, but I just stand here and look around at the empty room waiting to wake up from the nightmare that I'm surely having.

"Stay with me here, Jameson. We are going to find her. " Bones grabs my neck and squeezes trying to give me some strength.

"Prez." Yang calls for Archer who stepped back in the room with me.

"Yeah?"

"They didn't take her." Yang looked to him and then back to me. "Celine left on her own."

The rage quickly takes over. She didn't fucking leave. She promised me that she wouldn't leave. I trust that woman with everything I am and if she said she wasn't going to leave me than she wasn't going to fucking leave. "Fuck you, how the fuck can you say some shit like that? After all the shit that we have going on, you think we need to just dismiss the fact that she up and disappeared."

Yang took a step into my face, before inching back—a submissive gesture. Anger or not, I was still the fucking VP, his superior. I could be bat shit wrong right now and if he didn't speak to me with some semblance of respect, I could have his fucking hide. "Jameson, she left on her own. The alarm never sounded, because she disabled it. There is only one way to do that and it's from the inside. Unless you think one of those bastards walked straight through all of us and opened your door, picked her up without her saying a word and jumped out the fucking window." Yang points to the wires that should be attached. They aren't cut though, just simply disconnected and laid to the side gently.

He was right, she'd left on her own.

"This doesn't make any fucking sense, why the fuck would she leave now after she knows that we are going to protect her. Why the fuck would she leave me now?" I clench my jaw as a wave of unwanted fucking emotions threaten to render me useless. I was upset when I'd lost Monica, but that was more guilt and sorrow than anything else. Even in death I knew that we would never have been together and that she needed to stay out of my life. Except I was dumb enough to think that Celine was different. I'd believed that I could really trust her. Now I have to wonder if she has been playing us the entire time. Maybe she was in on this with Thomas and René. I've never once seen her father and it didn't make sense that he hasn't shown up anywhere on the fucking grid. Was she playing me from the start?

I grunt in frustration and sink my hands into my hair to pull on it. It does nothing to dull the ache deep in my chest. I roar out and swing with all my might into the nearest wall, over and over until I break a hole into the outer layer of wood and my hand strikes the cold metal underneath. Still, that doesn't stop me from swinging. The pain, maybe the pain can cut through the numb.

"Jameson! Fucking stop!" Archer tries to grab me, but I fling him off. The rest of the crew who was in the room step closer to me. Archer was the president, laying a hand on him wasn't allowed.

I stare at him laying there on the floor, "She fucking played us! She used me. I did this shit to my family for her and she fucking played me!"

"We don't fucking know that." Archer replies from where he is laying on his back. A flurry of guys come back upstairs, apparently their search of the clubhouse grounds is over.

"What's going on?" Shyne asks.

"Celine left on her own." Yang lets everyone know and they all huff out a breath like they have just been deflated. They have. They had thought she was family. Only for the woman I was fighting so hard to protect, turning out to be the fucking enemy.

"What the fuck? Why the fuck would she do that shit?" Clay says. Being a prospect, he shouldn't even be talking, but I don't have the mental capacity to correct him right now.

"This is bullshit. Fucking gashes." Pirate shakes his head and tries to walk away.

"No, you don't understand. She wouldn't do that shit." Clay continues to talk. "Jameson I was with her that night you guys were pinned down by René's men. She was willing to give up her own fucking life to make sure that you were ok. She ran in to a fucking fire fight to make sure that you were able to get out. If she did leave on her own there is more to the fucking story than her being a goddamn enemy ... because I don't believe that shit." Clay says, keeping my gaze. I hear him and everything in my fucking soul wants to believe that shit, but it doesn't make sense. I can't connect it to what I am seeing, because right now all I see is an empty room where she should be.

"Luke?" Daria's voice carries into the room.

"Daria?" Archer calls back, clearly worried that something is happening outside that he can't see.

Daria walks into my room with her laptop in her hands. She looks around to all the guys and then back to her husband. "I have something I think you need to see."

"What? Did they leave another message on the fucking page?" Archer gets off the floor.

"No, not them." She looks around the room again and then back to Archer. She needs his permission.

"It's ok. Show us." He says.

"Ok." Daria quickly drops down to the bed and opens the computer. "Celine and I had a conversation earlier about how I started dabbling into the dark web and all that stuff. I told her about browser histories and how most people don't realize that it doesn't really disappear. Just because you close something and open another page doesn't mean what you were originally searching for disappears." She clicks a few things and opens up the last page. It was about a gator hunting site and the next was about a meme. None of it made any sense.

"Are you saying she was looking for this?" Archer points to the screen.

"No, I think she wanted me to back track her browser history. I did. It takes me to her email. Usually I wouldn't open something so personal, but it felt like she was trying to send me a message or something." Daria back tracked a few tabs and finally made it to Celine's email. When she opened it up there were emails upon emails there. All of them with videos of a man being tortured. There is only one comment on each email. *One of yours, for what is mine.*

"Who the hell is that? You think that is her husband or something like that?" Pirate asks.

"What the hell, she isn't married man." I want to punch him in the face, but I couldn't deny the man in the chair looked super young.

"No, I think that is her father." Shyne says. He scoots forward on the bed trying to get a better look at what Daria is showing us and that slight movement causes my pillow to shift.

"Uh bro? What is that?" Yang says from where he is standing.

I turn my head to see him pointing at something on the bed. Holy fuck, it's a paper. She left a fucking note. I literally crawl my way through everyone not caring who I kick in the process to get over to that paper.

I can't help but smile and internally pump my fist to the ceiling in victory. She didn't leave me. She's a fucking dumbass. Thinking that she is doing something that is going to help us, but she didn't betray me like I was starting to think.

"What does it say? Judging by the smile on your face, she isn't a fucking spy or some shit like that."

"No, she's gone to get her father. She said she knew if she didn't show up, they would keep on hurting us. She wants to stop it. Give us a chance to hurt them for once."

"You have it, they left the address here." Daria turns the computer towards us, showing us the last email between Celine and whoever was sending the emails. "As long as they don't change location you should be able to catch up to them if you move fast."

I'm already out the door before Archer can give the order. My brothers are all on my hip too. Finally, we are going to be able to get some payback. I only pray that we get there in time to save my woman, even if it's only so I can shake some sense into her.

CHAPTER 27

JAMESON

The ride to what looks like an abandoned nightclub doesn't take long and from where we stash our bikes, we can see that it's not very heavily guarded. Or it could be and we just don't know. Shyne takes a step toward the building, but Yang grabs hold of him. He tells him to hold up, pulling him back to cover.

"You got a plan here?" Archer asks, his voice low as we all are in cover right now. Hoping that we don't give away our position or something like that.

"Look the last time we thought we had him cornered, his goons popped out of the wood work. I don't think we should go at him head on even if it does look like he is free and clear."

"From above?" Bones speaks up.

"How the hell are we going to do that shit?"

"You remember that fucking story I told you about Storm? If that bastard can jump from building to building so the fuck can we." Pirate smirks.

"Well didn't he lose you?" I poke fun at the man. There is a rogue member of our MC that we have all been searching for—Storm. His brother Vale has a fucking hit on his head, but Storm, we are not all sold on killing him. Apparently, Pirate saw Storm in town one day after he did a pick up and chased the bastard onto the roof. Where he promptly forced him to jump off the building. At least that is what Pirate says, I'd thought that maybe he just couldn't keep up with him in a foot race.

"Yeah, seems like the buildings are close enough together. I don't think they are going to be looking for an attack from above either. I agree, let's do it." Archer stands slowly and quietly makes his way to the side of the building. All of us crawl up the fire escape and just like we'd suspected there are more guards surrounding the place than we had first thought, but not many on the roof tops.

Archer taps my side and Yang's, then points to the two guards that are standing on the rooftop keeping watch. Fucking amateurs. They are stagnant and not really paying attention to everything that is around them. Someone could sneak right the fuck up on them and they wouldn't even know. That is exactly what Yang and I do. We quietly make our way up behind their backs and pull out our knives. Yang uses a quick slice across the man's throat while I jam my sharp knife into the small soft spot in the back of my guard's head. Both of them fall down to the ground quietly.

"You got to learn not to make such a fucking mess." I joke with Yang and he rolls his eyes at me.

He steps over the large pool of blood that is still leaking out of his already dead victim.

The rest of our brothers follow up behind us and together we jump to the roof of the building we believe they are holding Celine and her father in.

There is a skylight and I'm able to see what is going on inside. I raise my hand ready to punch my way through the glass pane, but Archer stops me. "Brother, we are too far up. You'll fuck yourself up and us if we fall."

"We have to find a way in there now!" I growl and look back down through the window.

There is someone holding her arms down. Thomas, that prick, is standing back jacking himself off. When he starts moving forward as if he is going to come at Celine, I feel myself losing my composure.

"We are going to get her out of there. We have to be smart about this though, the last thing that we want is to let either one of them get away. We have to end this shit now." Archer says to me and I have to take a deep breath, so I don't just jump through the fucking window.

"Shyne see if you can find a way in on the side, there has to be a walk way or something up here."

"Down on this side." Bones points to the other side and we all take off making sure not to bring any attention to us.

When we open the egress window, I can hear her screaming for the fucker to stop. I can hear her and all I want to do is fly down the fucking side of the wall and rip his fucking head off.

"Archer, take the fucking shot or I'm going to cause a fucking scene." I growl out slowly as my president holds up his weapon. Archer is one of the best marksmen alive, I should know I was his spotter for years. I know for sure that he can make this shot. It's everything else that is around us that can cause problems. We would deal with that after my woman was out of harm's way.

Archer inhales and holds his breath so that he doesn't move.

"They're here!" Someone screams from the side and before Archer can reset, he pulls the trigger. Thomas turns his head just as the bullet makes contact with his body. It pushes right through his neck and he falls to the floor, blood seeping out of the hole.

"Get the fuck down now!" I yell as all the guards that were hiding around the area begin to close in on us. There are definitely more guards than we'd thought. I'm counting at least 6 around us.

"Thomas!" René screams as he falls to the floor and attempts to go for his son. One of his guards holds him still as the bullets begin to fly all around. The group of us make our way along the small catwalk that encircled the entire club. We could have stayed up there and had the higher ground, but there was no real cover. They would only have to aim for a second and be able to take us out.

"Dad! Hold on!" Celine throws her feet up and kicks the man that is holding her down in the face, effectively getting him to let go. I see her crawl to the man that is nailed down to the table and turn them both over so they are as flat against the floor as they can be. The table the man is attached to falling down right along with them and providing great cover.

I stayed at Bones' three o'clock while Shyne was on his other side. Pirate was at our six and the rest of my brothers take up locations in other parts of the club where they would be able to shoot from afar. It didn't take long for us to clear the room of all of René's men, but by the time we were finished René had already escaped. His son was still alive and bleeding out on the floor from the wound to his neck. The bullet must have gone straight through destroying his voice box and the upper part of his esophagus. I assume it didn't hit an artery, because that would have killed him within seconds. He lay there on the floor, gagging and suffocating on his own blood. Red splatter pops up from his mouth every time he tries to take a breath.

"Where the fuck is your coward father?" Yang asks Thomas. I hope he doesn't give his father up. I would love to have Bones torture him for a few hours just to see what kind of information he is willing to give up then. Thomas reaches up to me and grasps at the fabric of my jeans. I kick his hands off of me. "Don't fucking touch me, you'll get no fucking sympathy from me. Or from any of my fucking brothers. After the shit you and your family did to ours, you should suffer a million times over." I suck up a huge glob of mucus from deep within my throat and spit it directly into his face.

Tears roll down his face as he tries to wipe it away. I bring my foot up and slam it down on his hand, breaking all the bones. I feel the bones crunch under my boot. He doesn't get to wipe it off, he needs to sit there and wallow in his fucking filth.

"I'm going to ask you one more fucking time. Where is your fucking father?" Yang demands.

Thomas turns his head to the side, but it doesn't look like he is doing it to ignore us. Its more as a way of telling us that his father is in that direction. Clay is the closest to the area that Thomas is gesturing with his eyes. Clay walks a few steps making sure to keep his gun drawn and eyes peeled. He steps forward a few times and then steps back once. Forward than backwards and once again moves forward than backwards.

"Archer." Clay calls out and when we all look towards him, he points down to the ground. The bastard is under the fucking floor.

All of us make our way over there surrounding what looks like a small door that is almost completely camouflaged in the ground. When Clay pulls the door up, René is under there with his gun pointed up. He pulls the trigger twice, but it doesn't fire.

"That's what you get when you have everyone else do your dirty work for you. Never fucking prepared." Archer grins down at the man.

"Prez." Clay calls out and shows us the grenade attached to his hip.

"Hell yes, blow him the fuck up." I say already excited that it was even a possibility. Fucking prospects, always running around with fucking bombs and explosives. I can't wait until we patch him in.

"Everyone else on board with that?" Prez asks.

A round of yeahs echo through us as Clay takes a step forward.

"Wait, wait. You know you don't want to kill me. That's not your fucking style. We can help each other out. I know all about your casino business. I can make it so that we are both very profitable from that venture."

"You think we would ever go into business with someone like you? You really don't know anything about the Wings. We don't give a fuck about the money. We don't give a fuck about what kind of fucking deal you can cut us. We care about the community and our fucking brothers. You can rot in fucking hell with your deal." Shyne snarls at the man.

"Fire in the hole!" Clay calls out and tosses a live grenade into the deep hole. We slam the door of the ditch shut and dive out of the way as a large explosion rattled the foundation of the nightclub.

I jump up and run over to the small hole. I open it and peer down into the smoke and rubble. Large slabs of rock and wood have broken free from whatever was under the building and is lying heavily on him. On one side I can see his legs are completely severed from his body. I don't want to go down there and check to see if he is still breathing though. Even if he is, he'll be dead before long from the extent of his injuries.

"Good shit boys!" Archer says as we all circle the hole and what used to be René.

"Is it over?" I hear Celine's voice ask from the other side of the area. The one voice that I swore was all I had wanted to hear and now that same fucking voice is filling me with rage.

CHAPTER

JAMESON

I turn in her direction and keep my gaze locked on her face. She bends down to try and help her father up from the floor even though he's still attached to the table. She tugs her shirt down trying to cover her bare bottom. Pirate takes off his shirt and she is able to wrap it around her waist.

"Who is that?" The man attached to the table asks.

"Dad, this is Jameson. He's my boyfriend."

"Am I? Is that what I am to you?" The words drip out of my mouth with disgust.

"Jameson, I had to do this. I had to ..."

"Bullshit!" I bark at her and she jumps back. "You didn't have to do this shit. You didn't have to put yourself at risk. We could have all come up with a better fucking plan."

"The plan worked." She shrugs.

"Yeah, barely. If we would have gotten here a minute fucking later ..." I clench my hands and exhale. I don't even want to think about what would have happened if we didn't make it. I know that my woman would never be the same if they took from her like that.

"I would have handled it." She squares her shoulders and takes a step towards me.

"Tell me how the fuck you would have handled it. What the fuck are you trying to fucking prove! That you are just as strong as one of us? That you don't need me? What the fuck is it?" I scream at her and

178

even her incapacitated father jerks in my direction as if he is going to try and defend her.

"No, Jameson." She softens and her hands go up to my neck, her fingers caressing my cheeks. "Jameson, this was never because I thought that I could do this without you or that I didn't need you. It's because I had to make sure you don't hurt anymore. He was taking too much from you. I'm never going to abandon you, but I won't leave you to fight your battles by yourself either. That is never going to happen with me. There was a way for me to stop him from hurting you, even if I failed there was no way that I wasn't going to try." She rubs her hands down my neck and let them fall to her side.

I want to argue with her and tell her that she shouldn't ever fucking do that again, but if I were being honest with myself, I would have done the same fucking thing.

"I love you Jameson. Even though we have been through hell and back, even though you get on my everlasting nerves with your over-bearing possessive self, even though there is still so much I need to learn about you and your family ... I love you. I don't want you to hurt."

I squint my eyes at her and do my best to keep the look of disdain on my face, but on the inside, I was dancing my best two step. She'd said she loved me.

Got her.

"You will never fucking do shit like this again, do you understand?" I grab her and pull her close to me.

"Can't guarantee it, but I'll do my best." She smirks at me.

"Uh ... I'm appreciative of you saving my daughter, but now that she is ok. If one of you could get this shit the fuck out of my hands that'd be great!" Her father snaps out.

"Oh fuck." Yang rushes over to help the man.

I wrap my woman in my arms, completely oblivious to the rest of my brothers running around gathering up all the dead bodies. I had more important things to deal with and that was loving on my woman.

"Jameson, what you want to do about René?" Bones asks me.

"Leave him to rot." I shrug and go back to Celine. Finally, it's over and I can get my life back on track with my woman—all fucking mine.

EPILOGUE

CELINE

Three Months Later-

"You're such a fucking cheater!" I yell out as Jameson tosses the football to Yang, who had to hold me down so he could catch the ball.

When I first met these men, I was sure I was leaving one bad situation for another. Only they have shown me first-hand what it's like to be a family.

They even welcomed my dad in the club. Of course, I wasn't expecting him to want to join up, but I guess him becoming a prospect for the Wings of Diablo is something that I'm just going to have to get used to. He'd spent all his young adult years making sure that I was taken care of. This was his time now and if he wanted to join this group, I was going to support him.

"Lex! You were supposed to hold your man!" Bones screams at my dad.

"Yeah dad!" I take my turn to yell at him in jest.

"Girl, I'm injured." He raises his hands. They were mostly healed up. He would never be the prized fighter he once was, but the damage wasn't nearly as extensive as we thought it would be.

"Oh please, how long you going to milk that shit?" Archer laughs as he runs by us.

We all move into our makeshift line as to set up for the next down. Jameson is the quarterback for the other side and Shyne is my team's quarterback.

Jameson calls for the faux snap and he steps back as the rest of his team runs a play in the small field that we created behind the club-house. I sneak to the side while he is still looking for someone to throw to. I catapult myself at him and he drops the ball to catch me. I sit on his chest and do a dance.

"Sacked!" I tease him.

He quickly rolls over and pins me underneath him. "I don't think that is proper form."

"I mean this is a team sport, you going to let all of us get in on that?" Bones says as he stops near us picking up the pigskin.

"Keep your fucking hands off." Jameson growls over my head, still as fucking possessive as ever.

"Celine, you trying to get me kicked out?" My father asks. I turn and look at him. I can't help but laugh. My father is a prospect so it means that he can't disrespect any of the patched members. Makes things difficult for him when Jameson likes to paw at me whenever he feels like it. He may be a prospect, but he is also my 37 year old father. The urge to beat the hell out of anyone who touches his little girl is still strong.

"Sorry dad." I try to push Jameson off and stand.

"I wonder what he is going to do when he finds out that you are moving in with me." Jameson kisses up the side of my neck and I shudder at the feel of it.

Once we made sure that there were no more people in René's orga-nization that were going to come for us, I left the clubhouse to help my father get back on his feet. Lucky for him, his years of conditioning as a boxer had allowed him to take beatings that a less fit man probably wouldn't have been able to endure. Sure, he had bruises with quite a few aches and pains, but they hadn't gone to town on him like I thought they would. Apparently, René didn't want to destroy his chances of getting back in the ring until that very last video. They had been taking it easy on him the entire time.

"Shh! He's going to flip out." I hush Jameson as I push him harder so I can get up.

Apparently three months is more than enough time for Jameson to figure out that he needs to feel me underneath him every night. From next week on, if he has his way, I will be a permanent resident of the Wings of Diablo clubhouse.

I look over my shoulder and wink at Jameson.

"Darlin' don't play with me." He stands up quickly and stalks after me.

It doesn't take much to rile him up. I can't wait to find out just how many ways this man can claim me. Body and soul.

EPILOGUE

RENÉ

"Guppie! Get your ass over here and give me some more fucking medicine! What the fuck are you good for!" I scream out in pure agony.

Sweat drips from my forehead soaking into my expensive pillows. When they said that they had to amputate more of my legs, I wasn't expecting this type of pain. I thought for sure that I would be over it in no time. I mean I had survived much worse. The explosion of the grenade took my left hand and a large portion of my forearm, severely disfigured my face and chest, the debris fallout was what took my legs. Large beams fell directly on top of my legs severing them on contact. It was those same beams that had actually saved my life. They pinned my legs down in such a way that it effectively stopped me from bleeding out.

I sat there in that hole for hours before one of my guards found me. When they did manage to get me out, I was barely hanging on to life. My soul died the second they pulled me out of that hole. I searched for Thomas, but the fuckers didn't even leave his body.

My other sons have tried to get me to forget about the Wings of Diablo and about that little bitch Celine, but I can't. I loved Thomas the most. He was like me in so many ways. Parts of him were better than I could ever be.

"Sorry sir, I don't want to give you too much. I know you are in pain, but I don't want to depress your respira-"

With my good hand I pick up my shit pan and throw it at him. Dark loose stool splashes his face and down the front of his shirt.

"Did I fucking ask you what you don't want to do? I said that I want more fucking medication. Give it to me now!"

He clenches his jaw and nods once. He cleans himself off quickly before coming back over to my bed and gives me the medication.

"Father, just take it easy. You don't need to rush. We are going to take care of everything." Ranger, my middle son calls out from the corner where he is keeping watch. I didn't bother to respond.

I believe my kids would do everything in their power to make sure that the business would stay up and running. Only they didn't understand that I didn't give a fuck about the business anymore. Those fucking biker assholes took something from me that I would never be able to get back. If it takes the very last fucking breath I have, those motherfuckers will pay for what they've done.

NEXT UP IN THE WINGS OF DIABLO!

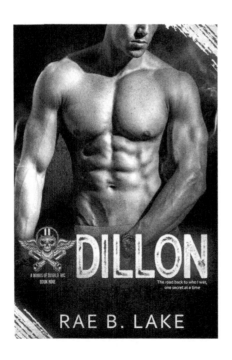

I've lost my way.

That much is clear.

I've spent so long as Wire, ruthless and cold-hearted as an MC president, that I can't see anything else.

Traitors tore my family to shreds and I was the one to let them in.

I turned a blind eye to the fucked up shit that was going on inside my club, and I was the only one who could make it right.

After I got revenge I knew I would never be able to fix what I destroyed.

Not as Wire.

Not as the president of the Wings of Diablo.

Turning Nomad was my only choice.

The empty road, my bike, and an occasional bottle of bourbon as my therapists.

The best medicine to keep the crippling guilt and failure at bay.

I can't run from my problems, or club, forever though.

This time... when I come home to face my demons, will I be able to handle the MC life or will I fall back into the same trap as before?

MORE FROM RAE B. LAKE

Tex
Maino

Juric Crime Family
Sven's Mark

Eve's Fury MC
Becoming Vexx
Free
Riot

The Shop Series Books
His Georgia Peach
To Protect and Serve Donut Holes
On The Edge of Ecstasy
His Peach Sparkle

Royal Bastards MC
Death & Paradise

Standalones
Drunk Love
Saving Valentine

FOLLOW RAE EVERYWHERE!

FACEBOOK
READER GROUP
TWITTER
INSTAGRAM
GOODREADS
AMAZON
WEBSITE
BOOKBUB
NEWSLETTER